Beverly Shorthair
New York
René Siamese
California
n the world wear REXLON

CATMOPOLITAN® *now*

Cover Look

Photograph of Pawlina Purrzikova by Francesco Scatvullo. Hair by Howard Furgler for Roger Tomcat for Burmese. Makeup by Fran Cooncat for Estée Longhair: "Wild Cat Purrple" Claw Enamel. Green Lamé Dress by Norma Katmali for On Meow Own. Necklace by Catier. Styled by Puss N. Boots. For Profile of Pawlina Purrzikova, see page 14.

▲ ***Beauty Mews***

Departments

6 Pad Into My Parlor
• *Havana Purrley Brown*

10 On Meow Mind: Reflections on the Morning After • *Persian Passion;*
Why Do They Call Us Finicky?
• *Mavis Manx*

12 Ima Katz's Anxiety Column

16 Books • *Carol E. Ragdoll*

18 Movies • *Rex Cat*

20 Music • *Kat Stephens*

22 Fat Cat's Notebook
• *Catherine Himalayan*

24 Cat Body • *Susan Ocicat, D.M.V.*

26 Cat Travel Update • *Roberta American Wirehair*

28 CATMO Horoscope • *Star Sphynx*

32 Cat Health Memo: News from the Veterinary World • *Maine DeCoon Cat*

58 CATMO Tells All • *Bombay Creature, Susar Somali, Laurence P. Malayan, and Susan Korat*

Fiction

90 *Hollywood Housecats* (Novel Excerpt)
• *Jackie Collars*

Articles and Features

34 Paws to Catch Your Breath—Cathletics and Feline Fitness • *Javanese Fonda*

38 Copy Cats—Pussy Pawtraiture
• *Art American Shorthair*

42 Pussies Galore—Feline Figurines and Cat Collectibles • *Siamese Statue*

44 Getting Your Claws Into Mr. Right? Rate Your Erotic Purrsonality (Quiz)
• *Raquel Rex*

48 CATMO Talks to Morris the Cat
• *Tabby Thompson*

50 Catatonic Catastrophe! Catnip—The Drug Problem • *Javanese Junkie*

52 The Cat's Out of the Bag—He's Pussyfooting Around • *Tiffany Traveler*

54 What Gives Me Pangs of Guilt? (Roundup)
• *Cymric Conscience*

72 Good Mousekeeping • *Matt Malayan*

74 Playing Cat and Mouse • *Tonkinese Toys*

76 Scratch 'n' Sniff • *Claudia Chartreux*

84 Welcome to the Rat Race: The Business Animal in the Corpurrate Battlefield
• *Gloria Snowshoe*

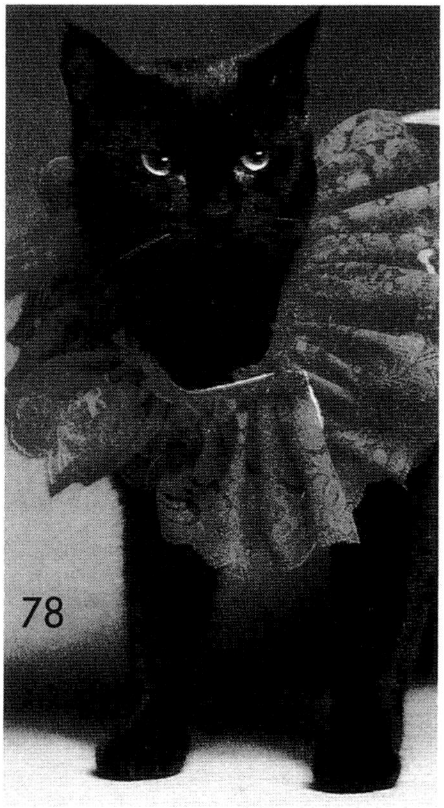

▲ ***Boudoir Beauties***

Celebrities

37 The Cat's Meow Right Now: Garfield
• *Japanese Bobtail Davis*

70 The Tomcat—What Can She See in Him? (The Centerfold of Burmese Reynolds)
• *Loni Abyssinian*

Beauty and Fashion

56 A Tale of Two Kitties—A Cat Can Change Her Spots in 3 Easy Steps!
• *Vidal Sinapura*

57 What's Mew in Beauty?

78 Fashion: The Cat's Pajamas—Feline Fashions Slip Out at Night • *Nancy Birman*

86 Fashion: A Cat's Nine Lives—Colorful Collars to Catch His Eye!
• *Nancy Birman*

Food and Decorating

46 Food: Cat Sup • *Pat Scottish Fold*

64 Decorating: Cat Naps—The Paws That Refreshes
• *Pat Scottish Fold*

66 Decorating: Cat Houses—Sleep with the Best
• *Pat Scottish Fold*

▼ ***Collar Creations***

WHICH CLAW IS THE SHARP ONE?*
Cover Cat ClawSlicks
5 FL. OZ
Claws that look sharp, because they are.™
Cover Cat®
Kitty Brinkley is wearing Pink Paws.

* All of them!

THIS IS YOUR MOMENT TO BE
P U R R

F E C T
PURRFECT
ESTĒE LONGHAIR
ECT
WEST FRAGRANCE FROM
ESTĒE LONGHAIR
NEW YORK • LONDON • PARIS

Clockwise from top right: Miami Vice, Burmese Reynolds, Havana Purrley Brown, Siamese Statue

☐ Cats are my favorite species. Yours, too? We are a most wonderful and mysterious group of animals. Our intelligence far surpasses that of the dog. People have finally begun to understand our superiority and desirability as companions. This year, statistics have confirmed that we are, in fact, man's best friend. We reside in more American homes than any other house pet, and we now outnumber dogs by more than 5,000,000; 56,500,000 of us live with American families, as compared to 51,000,000 dogs. Roll over, Fido! The cat is here to stay!

It is for this reason we present an article of interest to cat-loving people, as well as to cats, in this issue of CATMO. Normally, we restrict our coverage to areas of interest to cats, but in deference to people (who now hold us in such high esteem), we have included an article here for them. "Pussies Galore" by Siamese Statue is our valentine to people. The author has done extensive research into the human giftware market to unearth a multitude of unique and beautiful gift items featuring a cat motif. We do not present this story, however, without a small ulterior motive. It is our hope that people will purrchase these items as gifts—for us! (Pretty cagey, that Siamese Statue, to lend a helping paw to people in need. Especially if some deserving cat somewhere will be the recipient of a person's goodwill—and Siamese's good taste!)

The curvaceous and beautiful actress Loni Abyssinian provides a glimpse into the head and heart of her honey, the famous actor Burmese Reynolds. She gives us a glimpse of more than his psyche—we get to see quite a bit of his physique as well! CATMO, and Loni, present you with a story certain to live on in your memory for years to come—and a tear-out poster certain to live on your wall as long as it lasts! We're refurring to "The Tomcat—What Can She See in Him?" with the fabulous centerfold of Burmese Reynolds.

Cats are naturally sexy animals. We are known for our seductive walk, and the term "cat's eyes" means more than just a casual glance. Why, then, do some unlucky kitties have such trouble with finding, and keeping, a tomcat? Perhaps they're not setting their sights (those riveting cat's eyes) on the right cat! This month's quiz has been written by a famous sex kitten, the passionate Raquel Rex. Her name is synonymous with seduction, and if anyone is equipped to pen our test of animal magnetism, it's Raquel. "Getting Your Claws into Mr. Right? Rate Your Erotic Purrsonality"—take this quick quiz, and see whether top cats or alley cats are receiving your sex signals.

Fit felines are the wave of the future. Fat cats are singing the blues over their loss of status. Don't resign yourself to a life of sitting at home on Saturday nights eating mouseburgers! Take the tiger by the tail and change your shape, and your life. Javanese Fonda, the guru of feline fitness, shares her plan for losing weight and gaining popularity. She offers several options to help you regain your kittenish figure. One plan is sure to work for you.

I recently had the opportunity to attend a gala affair to benefit needy and homeless cats. I am refurring to the First Annual National Morris Awards Dinner. Sponsored by that famous feline philanthropist, Morris the Cat, and 9-Lives Cat Foods, the spectacular evening was a formal dress affair. The party was held at the well-known New York night spot, The Cat Club, and was the grand finale to preliminary Morris Awards given at local cat shows to mixed-breed cats. This final contest would choose the best mixed-breed cat in the country, to be selected from a group of those earlier winners. And what an evening it was! An extravagant show—kitty glitter! The winner was Miami Vice, a black-and-white shorthair.

I congratulate her, and all the other local winners, for proving my theory, the one that lies behind CATMO and is, in fact, my own purrsonal philosophy. "It's not what you have; it's what you do with it!" You don't have to be a great beauty to succeed. Any cat can achieve success if she sets her mind to it. Hard work goes a lot further than good looks. Do the best with what you've got! So with that thought, don't sit home eating mouseburgers. Get up and get going. And, most of all, have fun, my dears!

HPB

PAD INTO MY PARLOR

CLAWNIQUE
glossy claw enamel

C' L A W
PARIS

R É A L®
NEW YORK

I
hate
being
scratched
off.

And
I'm not
a cranky
cat.
Except when
my claws get
scratched.

So I use
C'Lawréal
scratch-
proof
claw enamel.

With a
little care
I can go
for days
with hardly
a scratch.

'bout time.

**Scratch-Proof
Formula
Claw Enamel.**

C'LAWRÉAL

Reflections on the Morning After

By Persian Passion

☐ I awaken from a romantic dream. The details are already beginning to blur, but I recall a violent night of passion. Bodies locked together in a fierce embrace. Waves of ecstasy. And pain. The cycle seems to repeat, over and over. I don't remember his face. Was it round and gray? Or lean and tan? Did he have a dark mask? Was his hair long or short? Now I am fully awake, and I attempt to recollect the nocturnal images more clearly. What was his name? Was he someone I know?

I stretch my whole body, and I am instantly aware that I feel different. A dull ache alternates with a feeling of well-being and satisfaction. What a strange combination! I can hardly remember the last time I felt this way. It must have been long ago.

The fog in my head is completely gone. The recollections come to me more quickly. It was not a dream at all. I have just awakened from a long-awaited evening of bliss. The destiny of our bodies meeting. The touch of his paws. A suggestive glance. A seductive cry. I abandoned all self-control and embraced him with a wanton lustiness that surprised me.

He clasped the back of my neck, and my body grew limp. Suddenly, I was engulfed with all of him. His paws were everywhere. Breathlessly I enjoyed his aggressive explorations. My body tingled to the tips of my fur. And then pain. Searing pain. I shook him aside and cried aloud.

I withdrew to a quiet corner of the room to catch my breath, but it wasn't long before the next one approached me. The gestures were the same. The excitement was still there. But after several more partners, I began to question the emptiness of these encounters. I was confused. My body sought further pleasure while my spirit cried out for a more meaningful relationship.

Toms, so many toms. My life seems to follow a cycle of abstinence and promiscuity. I am overcome by powerful urges beyond my control, and I am helpless. I wish I had more moral strength to ignore the handsome face and the compelling invitation, but the waves of passion are too strong to resist. And I comply.

It would not be so bad if my regrets were confined to a single weekend, but the effects of my actions are always far-reaching. Once again I will find myself pregnant and alone. Another litter of unwanted kittens will fill the laundry room, and my people will again be faced with more mouths to feed, more homes to find. Perhaps this time they'll take the effort to have me spayed, so that I can at least engage in safe sex, or no sex.

But for now, I will take a long and luxurious tongue bath and await the arrival of my faceless lovers. The weekend has just begun.

Why Do They Call Us Finicky?

By Mavis Manx

☐ "Mavis! Mavis, where are you? It's time for dinner, and I'm making your favorite meal. It's chicken, and I know how much you love it. Now, come out and have something to eat. It's almost ready."

I opened one eye and glanced sideways toward the kitchen. She'd probably keep me waiting again. I squeezed my eye shut and tried to recapture the fleeting dream that had just begun when I was jarred awake by her grating voice. I had been purrsuing a plump mouse across the kitchen floor when he scampered right into my dish. I was hovering over the dish, about to make my move when...

"Mavis, did you hear me? It's dinner time, and it's chicken. Your favorite. Please come and eat. You can be *so* finicky sometimes. Why, you'd think that I didn't take the time to feed you all your favorite foods. Imagine what it would be like if you had to take care of yourself. You'd have to find your own dinner, and make do with table scraps. Or mice. You'd have to catch your own mice! Now, how would that be? Just mice, and no tasty chicken. No, you wouldn't like that at all! So come here and eat your dinner."

What did *she* know? I would have *preferred* mice to chicken. Any cat would. People have such strange taste. But I *was* hungry. And with no mice in sight, I'd have to make do with her meager offerings.

My ears pricked up when I heard the kitchen cupboard swing open. I tiptoed into the kitchen, so as not to appear overly anxious. Dinner time had *finally* arrived. I stood beneath a chair, reluctant to be seen, and watched quietly as the woman placed the can of cat food under the blade of the can opener. The familiar whirr of the gears made my mouth water. I held my breath as she opened a drawer to remove a spoon. Slowly, far too slowly, she scooped the mixture into the china dish with my name on it. A quick turn of the tap produced a dish of cool water to accompany my meal. I began to lick a paw nervously in anticipation of the culinary delights that would soon await me. Would she never set down that dish? Finally, after an interminable wait, she placed both dishes on my mat; first the food, then the water. I heard her call my name, but I pretended not to hear. We can never let them think they have the upper hand.

She left the room, perhaps to find me, and I stepped slowly from the shadow of the chair. Silently, I approached the pair of dishes to examine more closely the evening's fare. One sniff, then another, confirmed that it was chicken again. And I hate chicken. When would she ever learn? I turned from the dish in disgust to calculate my next move.

If I *ate* the chicken, she would never know how much I loathed it. She might even, in her foolishness, think that she had finally stumbled upon the one food I liked best! And then I would have to endure the torture of facing a dish full of chicken day after day. No, that would never do.

If I *didn't* eat the chicken, however, I might grow weak from hunger. Lord knows, I hadn't seen a meal since last night, and I was already feeling light-headed from lack of nourishment. Without a meal, and soon, I would surely faint, perhaps even expire. Then wouldn't she feel guilty? A sinister smile began to cross my face, until I realized the repercussions of this possible ploy. *She* would feel guilty, but *I* would feel *dead!* No, that certainly wouldn't do. It would be far too drastic a move for far too little result. I would have to think of something else.

Now, if I ate *part* of the chicken... that might get my message across. If I nibbled delicately around the edges, I could relieve my hunger (and *live*), and she might not even notice that some of the food had been eaten. Especially if I smoothed down the edges with my tongue. (I knew that years spent licking my fur just so had developed my tongue into the sensitive instrument necessary to complete this task successfully.) Yes, *that* was the answer. Eat just enough food to get by (well, maybe a little more if it didn't taste *too* bad), and then pose dramatically on the sofa to create the desired effect: a frail and fading feline, moments away from starvation. She might even rush in with a can of tuna to revive me. *That* would teach her. She'd never call me *finicky* again. *Demanding*, perhaps, or *discriminating*. But never *finicky*.

The Metropolitan Museum of Art, gift of Mrs. Francis Ormond, 1950. (50.130.129)

ima katz's ANXIETY COLUMN

Q. I am a three-year-old American shorthair. I live in a suburban house with a nice family. I have free access into and out of the house at all times via a pet door that I can push open at will. I find that I enjoy the outdoors and spend a good deal of time outside when the weather is good. I guess that I'm a pretty lucky cat, but my problem is indirectly related to my good fortune. I recently came into heat for the fourth time. Unlike the three earlier occasions, when the family confined me indoors, this time they neglected to secure my pet door. I was overcome by strange sensations that were difficult to understand or control, so I sneaked outside. I was there for only a few minutes, rolling in the grass, when a handsome tomcat from down the street dropped in. I had seen him before, a tall, dark and handsome Burmese, but on that afternoon he looked especially good to me. He called out my name, and used some dumb old line (I think it was "What's new, pussycat?"), and, whoa! I was hooked! He had never really noticed me before, although I admit I've had my eye on him, so I was flattered by his sudden interest. He came up behind me and in spite of my last-minute (and halfhearted) attempts to scare him away, he soon had his way with me. After several more sexual interludes, he grew bored and went home. I'm afraid that I am now pregnant, and it's all too clear that he has no interest in me or our expected kittens. My family is unaware of my predicament. I'm in a terrible mess. What should I do?

A. This is no time to be a scaredy cat. You have to tell your family about your condition before the cat's out of the bag, so to speak. Before long you'll be hearing the patter of little cats' feet, and as a single parent, things will be easier for you if you have the love and support of your family. If they truly love you—and I suspect that they do, judging by the freedom they afford you—you can depend on them to be there for you when you need them. Your family will also prove to be invaluable in the special care they will give you prior to, and after, the blessed event. Tney can even be counted on to feed and look after your youngsters after you are back on your feet. Mothering is a full-time job, but you will appreciate a few moments for yourself every now and then. Finally, your family can also be helpful in locating good homes for your kittens after they are ready to leave your side.

Good veterinary care is expensive, but it is a small price to pay for the safety and security of your kittens. Inoculations against feline diseases are important for all newborns, and I trust that your family can be counted on to provide this care for your offspring and yourself. In addition, you should explore the possibility of being spayed after you deliver your kittens. One unwanted litter is a mistake your family will learn to overlook in time, but a repeat of this incident is unlikely to be looked on favorably. Good luck to you and to your whole kitten caboodle.

Q. I am a mixed-breed tabby cat. I live in the country on a farm. I try to pitch in and help the people I live with as much as I can. I am particularly good at keeping the barn and house mouse-free. I do this because I am good at it, but also because people seem to have trouble dealing with rodents. They use strange, primitive devices baited with cheese, but any smart mouse can easily remove the cheese without getting caught. The people are always talking about "building a better mousetrap," but I have yet to see it done correctly. I don't know why they spend time in this fruitless pursuit when their time could be better spent *growing* fruit. Leave the job to the professional, I say.

Anyway, I am writing to you because I don't understand how people think. I bring the farmer's wife all my good, dead mice, and what does she do but scream. One time she even jumped onto the kitchen table when I dropped a half-dead mouse at her feet! I can't understand why she did this. He was an especially tasty morsel—I ate him myself after he had lain untouched for over an hour. Why, he had even gotten cold! I don't understand how she could waste such a delicacy, and hurt my feelings by rejecting my gift.

A. People are strange animals. Not only do they waste time trying to develop a better mousetrap—they also spend untold millions attempting to create the perfect cat food to appeal to the highly discriminating cat palate. Why don't they just *ask* us what our favorite flavor is? I'm sure that it would be *mice*, paws down! *I* don't understand why they can't package a range of gourmet cat foods to appeal to our taste rather than their sensitivities. Minced mice would be a delicious entrée, followed by mouse mousse for dessert.... But people seem to have trouble dealing with mice. They are apparently not sophisticated enough to appreciate mouse flavor, but really, who's complaining? That leaves more mice for you and me. See what happened when they discovered tuna? They began to can all the choicest morsels for themselves, leaving us with the edges and the ends—tuna parts, as it were. So be thankful that people are peculiar and don't know a good thing when we seize it.

Q. I should probably consider myself very lucky. I have the good fortune to live with wealthy people in a beautifully decorated penthouse apartment in New York. I am surrounded by priceless art and antique furniture. My days are spent lounging on the satin cushions on my bed, lapping cream from a crystal bowl. I guess that I am one of the crème de la crème. While many would envy my life, I find it boring and unfulfilling. What can I do to give my life more meaning?

A. You might try to follow the lead of many other felines like yourself and go into philanthropy. There are many excellent and worthy cat causes that could benefit from your helping paw. Even if you are too lazy to take an active role as an advocat for these causes, you could still do your part by donating funds to these feline foundations. Fat cats have a tendency to grow lazy and content, and to forget the plight of their less fortunate fellow cats. The needy and homeless are only two of many causes that can use your help. So volunteer your services today. I'm sure you'll find that by helping the world become a better place, your life will take on a new purrpose.

Q. I am a good-looking cat with long red hair. Maybe I am too good-looking for my own good! I seem to attract the attention of a lot of tomcats. The trouble is, I'm a cat-tease and I lead many of these toms

on. I usually stop flirting just before it gets dangerous, scaring them off with a nasty swipe of my paw. On several occasions, however, I have let things go too far and have found myself the victim of a gang bang! I guess I'm just a promiscuous puss. What can I do to change my wildcat ways?

A. I hate to be catty, but from your letter it seems that you get what you deserve. A seductive cat walk will attract any tom out for a little tail. You're certainly getting your share of attention. My only recommendation is a rather drastic one, I'm afraid. The best way to turn off the toms is to turn off your engine. I'm suggesting that you take your kitty car to the vet for a tuneup. Get spayed before it's too late and you find yourself filled up with kittens!

Q. I share my home with two people and a dog. The people and I originally lived alone, but two years ago the dog arrived, and never left. I guess he's a permanent boarder. I have a sneaking suspicion that they invited him to live with us to keep me company! (I hate to admit it, but sometimes, when we've been alone all day, I *do* enjoy his presence.)

I have recently begun to notice that the people treat him differently from me. And *we* seem to react differently from each other even in the same set of circumstances! They will reprimand him more for behavior that they find unpleasant. They are unhappy if he jumps onto the chair or sofa but tolerant of these very same actions when I'm the one doing them. They never seem to tell *me* what to do (and I wouldn't listen to them if they did), but they're constantly barking out orders and commands to him. *I* would never tolerate that kind of treatment from people, but he not only tolerates it—he actually seems to welcome it! He is only too happy to obey their orders; and their requests seem to increase, rather than decline, in proportion to his eagerness to please them.

I, on the other hand, am free to explore every corner of the house. No room, or piece of furniture, is off limits to me. Oh, they may occasionally try to shoo me from their favorite chair, but seconds later I can return—and do—with immunity. In fact, they seem to expect my sudden reappearance. I would even go so far as to say that they respect my independence, and even envy it.

Why are we so different, and why do they treat us in this dissimilar manner?

A. The reason for the disparity in treatment is really quite simple. In this cat-and-dog life, dogs are treated like dogs. People attempt to make dogs conform to an unnatural standard of behavior. They expect dogs to be obedient and subservient to their commands. And dogs are happy to comply. Dogs, by nature, are pack animals who look to their leader for direction. In your home environment, the people have assumed the role of "lead dog," and your canine friend is only too happy to abdicate control and submit to their direction.

You, on the other hand, descend from a proud breed of intelligent and independent thinkers. Cats are solitary animals and do not follow orders dictated by a leader. We are free to form our own opinions. The only commands we follow are our own. Sure, people may try to trick or control us through subtle manipulation involving fear or food, but our minds remain clear, and we are free to change our behavior as the mood strikes us. People acknowledge and value our autonomy, and encourage us to express ourselves through actions that may be unpredictable but are always respected.

FAST AND FELINE. NEW ABYSSINIA ONE COAT CLAWCOLOR.

It's here. All the kitty-rich color and shine you want in one fast-drying coat. And twenty-four scratch-proof shades.

THIS MONTH'S **catmo cover cat**

Pawlina Purrzikova

HOME: I was born in Czechoslovakia and was separated from my litter as a kitten. I was taken in by a kind family who took me to Sweden with them when they fled the Communists. There, by chance, I was reunited with my mother!

AGE: 4

HEIGHT, WEIGHT, ETC.: I'm 1 foot tall, 19 inches long, and weigh 10 pounds. I can eat whatever I want because I get a lot of exercise chasing mice and climbing trees. I guess I'm just a country cat at heart!

BEAUTY ROUTINE: I have no special beauty hints. I just believe in eating well and keeping my fur scrupulously clean—I'm always licking a paw when I have a free moment.

GETTING STARTED: I never planned to become a model; it just seemed to happen. I was living a haphazard existence, catch as cats can, when I was discovered. I was working in a restaurant at the time, waiting under tables to catch mice. A talent scout from a famous modeling agency, Furred, came in to have lunch, and found me instead! She purrsuaded me to try modeling, and before too long, I found myself on the cover of *Harpurr's Bazaar*! I could hardly wait to place a pussy-to-pussy phone call to my mother to tell her the exciting news! We're very close—I used my first big paycheck to purrchase a new cathouse for her.

FAVORITE PASTIMES: I live in New York so I spend a lot of time at my window, watching the birds go by. I love to spend long weekends in the country, scratching trees and smelling the earth. It brings me back to my roots. I'm not very social, but when I get together with friends we eat a little catnip and occasionally chew some grass—I'm not one of those wild party-cats.

WHAT NEXT? I have just completed work on a new movie called *Anna and Her Kittens*. It was my first film and I'm proud of my purrformance. I would love to meet the right tomcat and settle down and have a family, maybe a litter or two. My dream is to have a barn in the country and fill it up with kittens, the whole kitten caboodle!

—Irene Colorpoint

Sharp Claws Begin with Develop 18

The Sharp Idea
For claws to be sharp, they must first be strong. Develop 18 was created for cats with sharp claws and for cats who want them. Develop 18 combines a product that works with a program of claw maintenance to help cats grow 18 sharp, strong, powerful claws. The kind of claws that look well, and work!

Develop 18 Works
Crystal-clear Develop 18 is used as a base and top coat. Protein fortifiers, vital conditioners, and claw strengtheners are formulated to help make Develop 18 work. Together, these ingredients help strengthen, reinforce, and prevent molting. And, with Develop 18, claw polish lasts longer, shines more, and stays scratch-free.

A Simple Program
The Develop 18 Program Guide and Survival Plan begins with the Claw Care Program for cats who want to grow sharp, strong, powerful claws. Every day you add a top coat of Develop 18 over claw polish. The Maintenance Care Program, with two applications a week, helps keep your claws sharp. The Survival Plan helps you break habits that break claws.

The Brand Name Purrfectionists Choose
Ask any claw care purrfessional to use Develop 18 as part of your grooming shop pawicure. And follow up at home with top coats of Develop 18. Or use Develop 18 as part of your at-home pawicure. Each day you use Develop 18, you are a day closer to sharper claws.

DEVELOP 18®
Where Sharp Claws Begin

BOOKS

By Carol E. Ragdoll

A COMPLETE CAT COMPENDIUM There is no better way to describe this comprehensive volume on cats. ***The Book of the Cat***, edited by Michael Wright and Sally Walters, was originally published in England by New Leaf Books Ltd. It has been released in America by Summit Books, and it is equally at home on either side of the Atlantic. This handsome trade paperback volume offers the cat and cat lover alike a broad examination of the cat from its evolutionary origins through the breeds of cats found today. Detailed chapters on The Breeds of Cats, Understanding Your Cat, Keeping a Cat, Your Cat's Health, and Breeding and Showing of Cats are explained in easy-to-understand language. The book is liberally illustrated with both line drawings and photographs to clarify and enhance it. This book is the purrfect gift for a cat who wants to understand more about her origins and life-style, or for any cat-loving person you may know (and there are *many* of them!).

DOMESTIC CATS EXAMINED Muriel Beadle's ***The Cat*** was originally published in 1977 by Simon & Schuster but is as popular and informative today as when it first appeared. Mrs. Beadle has written a lovely book that strikes just the right balance between scholarly research and pleasurable reading. She has drawn her research from a rich variety of sources. The wealth of information—from seventeenth-century naturalists to modern behaviorists, from memoirs of cat fanciers to scholarly reports, from specialists in fields as diverse as ecology and genetics, veterinary science and neurophysiology—is exciting and holds the reader's interest. This book deserves a place on any informed cat's bookshelves.

NO BAD CATS We always knew that, but Mordecai Siegal's book, ***The Good Cat Book***, reaffirms our belief. The book, published by Fireside Books, is a trade paperback volume that promises to teach people "How to Live with and Take Loving Care of Your Cat." It does. This beautifully organized volume is a complete how-to book for humans on how to live happily with a cat. It touches on many points that are sure to enhance the human–cat relationship. Mr. Siegal gives people basic information about cat care, tempered with delightful tidbits like games to play with your cat and dietary delicacies for fat cats (my favorite recipe here features shrimp). This book is directed at people, but it is equally informative for cats of all ages. It gives us a glimpse into how people think and what they feel is the proper way to live with us. It provides a new purrspective on our human companions, and reminds us that while cats and people may not always think alike, they usually do have our best interests in mind.

AILUROPHILES UNITE Roger Caras, a television news correspondent for ABC and an authority on pets and wildlife, has written more than fifty books on these subjects. His recent book, ***A Celebration of Cats***, published by Simon & Schuster, reveals him to be an ailurophile. No, it is not a dread disease. It means that he is a cat lover. This book may be viewed as his val-

entine to all of us. Just read it and feel the love. From his dedication to the thirty-one cats he has known and loved (and I may have to forgive him for giving away our secret by calling us closet smoochers), to his concluding sentence ("For if truth be told, and however impossible the idea, I would like to have known every cat that has ever lived"), Mr. Caras reveals a deep and abiding respect for the human–cat bond. In spite of the fact that he is a person, I would call him one of our staunchest advocats!

A FIELD GUIDE TO AMERICAN CATS. ***Simon and Schuster's Guide to Cats*** is a clear and concise paperback volume that helps you identify the 40 longhair and shorthair breeds found in North America. (The standards are dictated by the cat registry organizations in North America—European and other standards may vary from these). The book may be used to identify the physical and behavioral characteristics of each breed (so helpful when selecting a *mate*), or it may be read simply for pleasure. The breeds are illustrated with more than 200 full-color photographs, drawings, and symbols to make identification easy.

An informative overview of the history of cats, cat characteristics, and basic cat care is also provided. While this may appear to be an "owner's manual" for people who reside with cats, we prefer to view it as a basic field guide to all the cats in the field. It makes the chase easier when you can narrow down the field to those breeds that appeal most to you!

KATLÚA
&
cream
IMPORTED
FROM SUNNY MEXICO
KATLÚA
LICOR DE CAFÉ
LIQUEUR
Frrresh. Naturally more delicious because you make it yourself: with a splash of Katlúa to a dish of fresh cream, or milk, over ice. The cat's meow, right? Because only Katlúa tastes like Katlúa.

BOOKS *[continued]*

THE DOCTOR MAKES CAT CALLS...Dr. Louis J. Camuti not only makes house calls to visit his patients in familiar surroundings, he also makes cat calls when purrsuing a patient across her bedroom. ***All My Patients Are Under the Bed—Memoirs of a Cat Doctor***, by Dr., Louis J. Camuti, published by Simon and Schuster, is a warm-hearted book written by America's most beloved and prestigious cat doctor, who has been treating felines for nearly sixty years. Dr. Camuti shares with us his funny and tender tales of a multitude of cat patients and their people. There are celebrity cats (and cats who live with celebrities) and regular cats. Each has an original story to tell, and the doctor takes great joy in sharing these stories with us. He even reveals, for the first time, his famous "Camuti Method" for tracking down reluctant pet patients, even in their most ingenious hideouts (beds, linen closets, and even refrigerators!). We may find it hard to forgive him for this (how could he rat on his friends?), but with this one minor exception, the book is a joy to read, and we thank the doctor for his many years of service to the cat community.

MOVIES

By Rex Cat

NEW AND TOPS IN VIDEOCASSETTES

This month I'd like to take a departure from my coverage of new releases to devote the entire column to videocassettes. After all, with the exception of the few crafty cats who manage to slip into darkened theaters, how many of us are able to see the new films at movie houses? Very few, with the majority of us confining our viewing to videocassettes seen at home. Many films of particular interest to cats of all ages are currently available on tape. I am able to review only a small selection of them in this month's column, but plan to expand this feature in upcoming issues of CATMO.

© MCMLXXXV Walt Disney Productions

CAT CATHARSIS Elizabeth Taylor is steamy as Maggie the Cat in Tennessee Williams' prize-winning drama ***Cat on a Hot Tin Roof***. The film also stars Paul Newman as Brick, her husband, and Burl Ives as his father, Big Daddy, the family patriarch. The movie is a sizzling examination of the emotional, sexual, and political wars among a dying Southern mogul's heirs. Elizabeth Taylor is riveting as she claws and scratches for her last chance at a future that she desperately craves. ***Cat on a Hot Tin Roof*** is classic cinema that should be mandatory viewing for the CATMO Cat.

I loved almost everything about the film, but one basic question has been puzzling me for years. Why was the role of Maggie the Cat given to Elizabeth Taylor? I don't deny that she is a fine actress who was able to bring the role to life in spite of her obvious shortcoming—she is a *human* and not a *cat*. There are untold quantities of excellent cat actresses who would have given their eyeteeth for a chance to purrform the role of Maggie on screen. The film industry should try casting closer to type in the future, so that cats are given a fair opportunity to purrform and excel. ***Cat on a Hot Tin Roof***, MGM/CBS Home Video.

I TAWT I TAW A PUDDY TAT... Sylvester the Cat and Tweety Bird return in eight classic cartoons in ***Warner Bros. Cartoons Golden Jubilee 24-Karat Collection***. Sylvester and Tweety are just as you remembered them from kittenhood, and now they're available on tape to entertain a whole new generation of kittens. The eight classic favorites include the ever popular ***Mouse-Taken Identity*** and ***Hyde and Go Tweet***. My particular favorite is ***The Last Hungry Cat*** (but it is getting close to mealtime and Tweety is making my mouth water....). ***Warner Bros. Cartoons Golden Jubilee 24-Karat Collection***, Warner Home Video.

FUR WILL FLY ***Fritz the Cat*** is an irreverent look at the animated cartoon. The cartoon format lulls me into a false sense of security. I settle back into the cushions, ready to see some family fun. All those cute kittens and cats wearing clothes. When suddenly I look closer. What are they doing there? Where are their clothes? I've never seen a cat look like *that* before!

Fritz the Cat is definitely not for the Mickey Mouse set. This cartoon is X-rated. We see animated animals doing things we've never seen them do before! This film requires prior warning and a liberated attitude. The CATMO Cat will add this tape to her film library for those times when her tom needs some extra purrsuasion! ***Fritz the Cat***, Warner Home Video.

TOUCH YOUR CLAWS Cathletics will never be the same, once you've seen ***Mousercise*** by Walt Disney Home Video. You may be lazy and unmoved by standard video exercise fare like Jane Fonda, but I guarantee that ***Mousercise*** has what it takes to get you up on your paws and moving! This tape differs from all the others in the genre in featuring Mickey Mouse and his friend Donald Duck. While the exercises are a bit juvenile (this tape was designed for *children*, but don't let that bother you), the sight of our favorite (and tasty) mouse and duck will have you up and around in no time! Imagine, both a mouse and a duck—something for everyone! The laziest fat cat will be climbing the screen for this workout tape! ***Mousercise***, Walt Disney Home Video.

HISS
?
georges
mickeymouso

MUSIC

By Kat Stephens

A Singing Cat

PUSSY, THEY'RE PLAYING YOUR SONG. Pet Song is a unique business developed by musician and composer Dennis Knick. It offers us an unusual way to be immortalized in music. Pet Song will produce a cassette recording of an original song that incorporates your name and purrsonality traits. You may choose your favorite type of music (folk, rock, or country, although more unusual formats have been selected—classical and polka among them). After filling out a Pet Song Pet Profile about your habits, activities, and the traits that make you special, Pet Song will provide you with a unique, purrsonalized "theme song." The company has produced hundreds of these songs for many cats, dogs, and others. Each song is original and is recorded with vocals and full instrumentation. A lyric sheet is included. Dennis Knick of Pet Song has written a special song for CATMOPOLITAN; one verse appears below:

CATMOPOLITAN Meowsic

When I open the cover of CATMO
What do you think I see?
Everything you could want for your cat,
It's a Pussy Pawpourri.

In addition, they have produced a "Best of Pet Song" album of sorts.... *Pet Song Sing-A-Long* is a cassette tape that features eight songs actually commissioned by pet patrons. To order *Pet Song Sing-A-Long*, or a custom-written song, phone (312) 635-SONG or write to Pet Song, P.O. Box 463, Des Plaines, IL 60016.

FIRST THERE WAS MUZAK™, NOW THERE'S "PETZAK." You walk into the veterinarian's office and take a seat. While pawing through the last issue of ***Cats*** magazine you become increasingly aware of the familiar vocals from the sound system. Why, it's ***The Singing Cats!*** You listen more closely, and suddenly you hear Elvis singing ***"Hound Dog."*** When you finish reading the article on show cats, you recognize the voice of Carly Simon singing ***"Mockingbird."*** Where did all this animal-oriented music come from?

Is it a new radio station, WPET? No, the source of this exciting new background music is a cassette tape called "Petzak." Petzak is the animal answer to Muzak™—a 45-minute-long tape featuring songs about animals. All kinds of animals. A good number of the songs feature cats and birds, so your interest is sure to be piqued. The company behind this musical venture is called Innovative Amenities. They intend to market the tape to veterinarians, groomers, and other pet retail establishments. If they have their way, you'll be hearing a lot of this music as you purrform your daily errands! You can even order your own tape and play it at home! To order, contact Innovative Amenities, 1021 Lincoln Blvd., Suite 217, Santa Monica, CA 90403; (213) 394-6992.

THEATRE

NOW AND FOREVER—CATS

Inevitably, a musical about cats has become one of the most popular shows of all time. The phenomenally successful ***Cats*** had fairly modest beginnings. English composer Andrew Lloyd Webber, flush from the success of his early productions—***Joseph and the Amazing Technicolor Dreamcoat, Jesus Christ Superstar,*** and ***Evita***—decided to set a simple book of children's rhymes to music. The book, T. S. Eliot's ***Old Possum's Book of Practical Cats***, has been wholly transformed, via a $4 million production budget, into an exciting multimedia extravaganza. Utilizing the talents of multimedia director Trevor Nunn of The Royal Shakespeare Company, stage designer John Napier, choreographer Gillian Lynne, and a talented cast of thirty, ***Cats*** is spectacular—a must-see for the CATMO Cat! The play, which opened in London in May, 1981, was introduced to American audiences in early October, 1982. The Broadway production at the Winter Garden Theatre had advance sales of over $6 million. The hit song ***"Memory"*** has been recorded more than 600 times by a variety of artists (unfortunately, no cats have howled it so far). At this writing, the play has run for over five years in New York, six years in London, and in many other productions staged in countries as diverse as Japan, Hungary, and Germany. The slogan ***"Now and Forever, Cats"*** seems particularly appropriate when we realize that this success has been achieved in only *one* lifetime—and everyone knows that cats have *nine* lives!

© 1982 Al Hirschfeld. Drawing reproduced by special arrangement with Hirschfeld's exclusive representative, The Margo Feiden Galleries, New York.

MICRO-CHIP POLISH.
CATEX PERFECT COLOR FOR CLAWS
The new Catex micro-chip formula with
micro-chip sealers keeps Catex Purrfect Color for Claws
scratch-proof longer, even in the kitty car.
CATEX

Fake Claws Can Damage Your Paws!

Why? *Attaching fake claws with tape or glue can gum up paws and make them difficult to use, defeating the purpose of fake sharp claws.*

Now! Nutra Claw *Plus*™

A Veterinarian's Special Formulated Conditioner to Strengthen and Sharpen Your Own Claws, and a Plan to Prevent Fake Claw Damage!

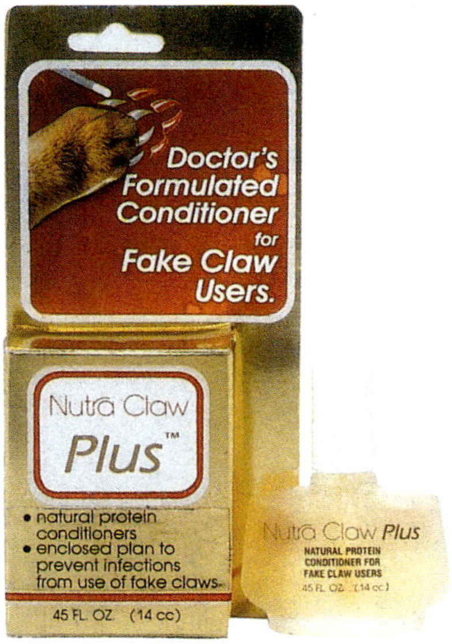

$1.00 REBATE OFFER Send us your old, sticky set of fake claws and we will send you a coupon good for $1.00 off your next purchase of Nutra Claw *Plus*.™ **$1.00 REBATE OFFER**

Name____________________________

Address__________________________

City_____________________________

State____________ Zip____________

This offer void where prohibited and expires 9/1/81
Please allow 6-8 weeks for delivery.

$1.00 REBATE OFFER **REBATE OFFER** **$1.00 REBATE OFFER**

FAT CAT'S notebook

By Catherine Himalayan

MAINTAINING YOUR FELINE FIGURE

If you are like most of us, you are pleased with the shape you are in (whatever shape that is). Most cats are looking for a diet strong in flavor, and if the nutrients are there, so much the better. Actually, cats have finely developed appetites and are very discriminating. Left to our own devices, most cats would prefer a meal of freshly caught game; mice, most birds, and insects are favorites. Most domestic cats, however, have little opportunity to catch our own food and we must rely on the prepared foods served to us by humans. If cats had their choice, these foods would resemble our natural favorites—mice would top the list. But human-food companies do not prepare packaged varieties of mice because people would find them unpalatable. People have strange tastes. To compensate for failing to serve our all-time favorite dish, the major pet-food companies have developed a full range of foods to satisfy any taste. People taste, that is. A typical supermarket that I visited recently stocked sixteen different brands of food in the three most popular forms: dry, moist, and canned. The canned foods offered the greatest variety: seventy-one different flavors at the supermarket I checked. No mice, but seventy-one possible substitutes. In all likelihood, one or two will be moderately pleasing to our taste. In fact, any cat can conceivably try a different brand and flavor every night for two months without having to repeat herself! And this takes into account only the brands sold in supermarkets.

Many fine foods are not available at the supermarket. These varieties are stocked at special pet-supply stores. They include special formulations for health and dietary conditions. Special reducing diets are also available here. With such a large selection, a cat would be hard-pressed not to find a food that satisfies her demands. (Major cat-food brands are listed in the box below.)

In spite of the vast variety of foods that are commercially available at both supermarkets and pet stores, some particularly selective cats will insist on eating a diet of foods freshly prepared in their own kitchens. Until kittens learn to cook, this idea is practical only if you can coerce your family into preparing such meals for you. Many kittens can. For these lucky kits, I can suggest several cat cookbooks. Among the best are:

1. The Cat-Lovers' Cookbook
written by Tony Lawson
illustrated by Paté Lawson
created and developed by Kingsley Barham
Storey Publishing
Storey Communications, Inc.
Schoolhouse Road
Pownal, VT 05261

2. The Kitty-Cat Cookbook
written by Barbara Ellen Benson
illustrated by Michael J. Rogers
Barrington Productions
P. O. Box 491300
Los Angeles, CA 90049

3. Cuisine for Cats
written by Richard Graham
illustrated by Don Grant
Pedigree Books
23 Wandsworth Bridge Road
London SW6, England

FOODS:

Supermarket Brands

Ralston Purina:
Purina Cat Chow
Meow Mix
Special Dinners
Thrive
Tender Vittles
Purina 100
Happy Cat
Alley Cat

Kal Kan:
Crave
Kal Kan

Carnation:
Friskies
Chef's Blend
Friskies Buffet
Fancy Feast

Nine Lives:
Nine Lives
Amoré

Pet Store Brands

Iams:
Cat Food
Kitten Food

Science Diet:
Feline Growth
Feline Maintenance

Purina:
Pro Plan Growth
Pro Plan Adult

Noah's Kingdom:
Best Cat Food

Cool
Cats of California

CAT body

By Susan Ocicat, D.M.V.

Q. I spend a lot of time bathing and licking my fur, even when it isn't dirty. I've noticed that I lick myself even more in the warm weather. Is this a bad habit, or is there a reason for it?

A. Your behavior is perfectly natural. All cats spend a lot of time licking their fur for hygienic reasons. It keeps the fur clean, removing the dust and debris that accumulate on your body from everyday wear and tear. Licking does a lot more than cleaning, however. It is essential during warm weather. You are depositing a fine layer of saliva over your body that then evaporates to keep you cool. In addition, your licking provides you with essential vitamin D, produced by the sunlight shining on your fur; licking the fur aids in assimilating the vitamin into your diet.

Q. I live in a suburban development with a tomcat. Indoors, he's a perfect gentleman and always uses our litter box, but outdoors he is a changed animal! While I eliminate discreetly in the yard, he makes a great show of spraying everything in sight—walls, trees, garden furniture. Nothing is safe! I know there are differences between males and females, and this is certainly one of them! Why does he do this?

A. Tomcats spray to mark their territory. Female cats, like you, do not have these urges. A tomcat likes to define his space and send out signals to other roaming cats that he has been there. These scent signals are very specific and reveal a whole range of information to the local cat population. By sniffing the marks of others, your friend can determine who has been in the area, how recently, and even the sprayer's emotional state. It keeps him informed of activities in the area and enables him to arrange his daily activities accordingly.

Q. I consider myself a healthy female cat with a normal sexual drive. I enjoy the game-playing and romance that make up cat courtship. And I certainly take great pleasure in the sexual act itself. Why, then, do I find the completion of the act so painful? I often scream out loud once the lovemaking comes to an end. What is my problem? Is it normal?

A. The reaction you are having upon withdrawal is perfectly normal, so don't be concerned. The male's penis has barbs that point away from the tip. Entry is easy; withdrawal is more difficult, as these barbs scratch the female cat as the penis is being withdrawn. This unpleasant reaction is necessary for reproduction, because the scratching sensation stimulates ovulation so that fertilization may take place.

Q. I live in an apartment and have little opportunity to go outdoors. I don't really miss being outside, but every now and then I get an overwhelming urge to eat the potted plants and chew on grass. I have tried to substitute other foods, but only grass will do. Sometimes I even throw up what I've eaten, but I can't control it. My family is disturbed by this seemingly destructive behavior, but I can't help myself. Why do I do this, and how can I stop?

A. Experts have explored this activity in many cats and have several possible explanations. Some feel that grass is a natural laxative and aids in removing hairballs from your system. A similar theory suggests that the grass promotes vomiting, as you describe. This is another effective (if unpleasant) way to eliminate hairballs. Finally, a majority of experts is convinced that the cause is a lack of several essential trace elements that are not part of your basic diet. The most important one is folic acid, which can prevent anemia. Your body is smart enough to detect this deficiency and it prompts you to take an unusual action to correct it. Whatever the explanation—and they are all plausible—do continue to follow your urges. Two tips—don't destroy the plants, and vomit discreetly in the litter box, not on the carpet or sofa!

Q. Whenever my people come home, I immediately run to them and rub my face and body up against their legs. They seem to enjoy this, and while I'm happy that they do, I don't understand *why* I always greet them in this way. Is it just the cat way of saying hello?

A. You may call it that, but the action you describe is more complex. What you are doing, without even realizing it, is marking the people with your personal scent. This makes them smell more familiar to you. Your face and the top of your head have powerful scent glands. These odors are recognized by cats but not by people. Coming home from the outside world, people carry with them the unfamiliar scents of the places they've been and the people they've seen. Your rubbing and stroking pick up and identify these scents, and once you've realized where they were and whom they were with, you "erase" these messages by imparting to them your own familiar personal scent. Thus, they become once again your own personal property!

Q. I'm not a bad cat, but I'm habitually drawn to my person's favorite chair. Not only do I sit and sleep on it whenever I can, but I have now started to claw the fabric. I began with a discreet corner near the back, where he didn't seem to notice. Recently, however, I got carried away, and today I've torn up the seat. He's sure to notice it this time! I'm writing this letter from the back of his closet, where I'll continue to hide until he forgives and forgets, or until I see your response and suggestion, whichever comes first! Why have I done this, and how can I get him to forgive me?

A. I'm afraid that the damage is done, in more ways than one. You have ruined your person's favorite chair. I cannot work miracles. It is unlikely that he will forgive you and let you continue your destructive behavior. He will probably take drastic action. By the time you read my response, you may already have paid a visit to the veterinarian and been declawed. While this sounds like a drastic reaction to the ruining of a chair, in the long run you may come to accept it. The actual operation is not pleasant, but you will recover and eventually forget it. And you can begin to rebuild the trust and friendship with your person.

In your defense, I will say that your actions were perfectly normal. Chairs are very tempting as scratching posts, particularly one so well cured with your person's scent. The scratching action sheds the dead sheaths from your claws and provides you with necessary exercise, but you have selected his favorite chair for a special reason. His scent permeates the seat and you are rubbing your scent onto his, from scent glands in your paws. In this way you have made his scent more familiar to you, and more tolerable to your sensitive nose. Once you have been declawed, you can continue to rub your paws on the seat, or anywhere else in the house, to mark your scent without ruining the furniture. In the long run, this may prove to be a workable solution for both of you.

The look Begins..with Maidenfur.
Start with Feline Fancies…
The satin and lace little nothings that make you feel furry under everything.

LYNDA CATTER

BEAUTY SECRETS

Q. My lashes seem skimpy. What can I do to make them look fuller?

A. Very little, because cats don't *have* eyelashes. You are probably mistaking the fine fur surrounding your eyes for eyelashes. You would be wiser to concentrate on accentuating your true beauty assets, such as your long eyebrows or full whiskers. These may be enhanced by careful grooming and regular application of emollient conditioners.

The right conditioner and the way you apply it can make all the difference. Here are some tips that should help.

As you apply your conditioner, move the brush in a slight side-to-side motion as you stroke upward or outward. This applies conditioner to every hair.

Another tip. Look for a conditioner that can be used for both eyebrows and whiskers. I think conditioning is most important if your hairs are thin or fragile, as most eyebrows and whiskers are.

Wonder Whisker® conditioner by Mewbelline is my favorite. It conditions eyebrows and whiskers, and is hypoallergenic and veterinarian-tested, so it's safe for use near the delicate eye area.

Lynda Catter
Fashion and Beauty Director

Mewbelline®

CAT TRAVEL update

By Roberta American Wirehair

Feeling Clawstrophobic?

It's time to get away!

Are you catatonic with boredom? Is the rat race beginning to get to you? You deserve a brief vacation, the chance to be whiskered away for some R&R (rats and relaxation). So make tracks for the nearest cattery or cat house—it's sure to bring out the animal in you!

Traveling with Your People

Ralston Purina has published a booklet with the odd misnomer "Traveling with Your Cat." An obvious mistake, which we have taken the liberty of correcting in our headline. Regardless of its title, the free booklet offers tips on how to travel with people, and it tells them how to plan for a trip that will be comfortable and enjoyable for *you.* The booklet offers suggestions for auto and air travel, hotel stays, and information on how to select a safe and comfortable cattery (should you choose to spend your vacation alone). The booklet is available from many veterinarians, or you may order a copy by contacting the Pet Information Center, 505 Market Street, Knoxville, TN 37902. This booklet is only one of a series called "Special Care for Cats." At least they got the name right *that* time!

Visit Ernest Hemingway's Cat House

Ernest Hemingway was a great lover of cats. Nearly fifty cats lived with him in his home in Florida's Key West. He provided for his feline friends and their descendants—many of those cats and their kittens still reside there long after his death in 1961. The house was opened to the public in 1964 so that fans and admirers of "Papa" Hemingway—world-famous author, Nobel Prize winner, bullfight aficionado, big-game hunter, deep-sea fisherman, world adventurer, and, most importantly, cat lover—would be able to visit the house at 907 Whitehead Street that he called home. The Ernest Hemingway Home and Museum is a registered national historic landmark. For further information, contact Bernice Dickson, 907 Whitehead Street, Key West, FL 33040.

Send Your People to a Cat House

The Anderson House in Wabasha, Minnesota, is a *real* cat house. People who come to stay at this cozy inn get to select a kitten of the evening. The hotel maintains a stable of warm and affectionate felines to offer its guests cat companionship with the purrsonal touch. This unique service began quite accidentally when a long-term guest asked if there was a cat at the inn that could keep him company. Word of this special roommate service hit the news media, and soon requests came in from other guests who wished to be provided with a cat for the night. The hotel was happy to comply, and today there are ten cats for the hotel's fifty-one rooms. Guests must reserve a cat early, as the demand far exceeds the supply. This unusual arrangement is heralded by cat lovers as providing *all* the comforts of home! To make reservations for your people, contact The Anderson House, 333 West Main Street, Wabasha, MN 55981, (612) 565-4524.

Travel to Houston to Purrchase Cat Gifts

The Cat's Pajamas calls itself a "complete place for cats." We tend to agree. This emporium offers the modern cat excellent hotel accommodations, the latest in beauty and grooming techniques, and a complete selection of cat goods for cats and their people. The cattery maintains the highest standards of cleanliness, and a veterinarian is always on call. A pick-up and delivery service to the airport is provided. Best of all, no dogs are allowed, so you won't suffer the trauma of constant barking, which is a hazard at some other boarding facili-

[continued on 49]

Join the book club that's as catmopolitan as you are.

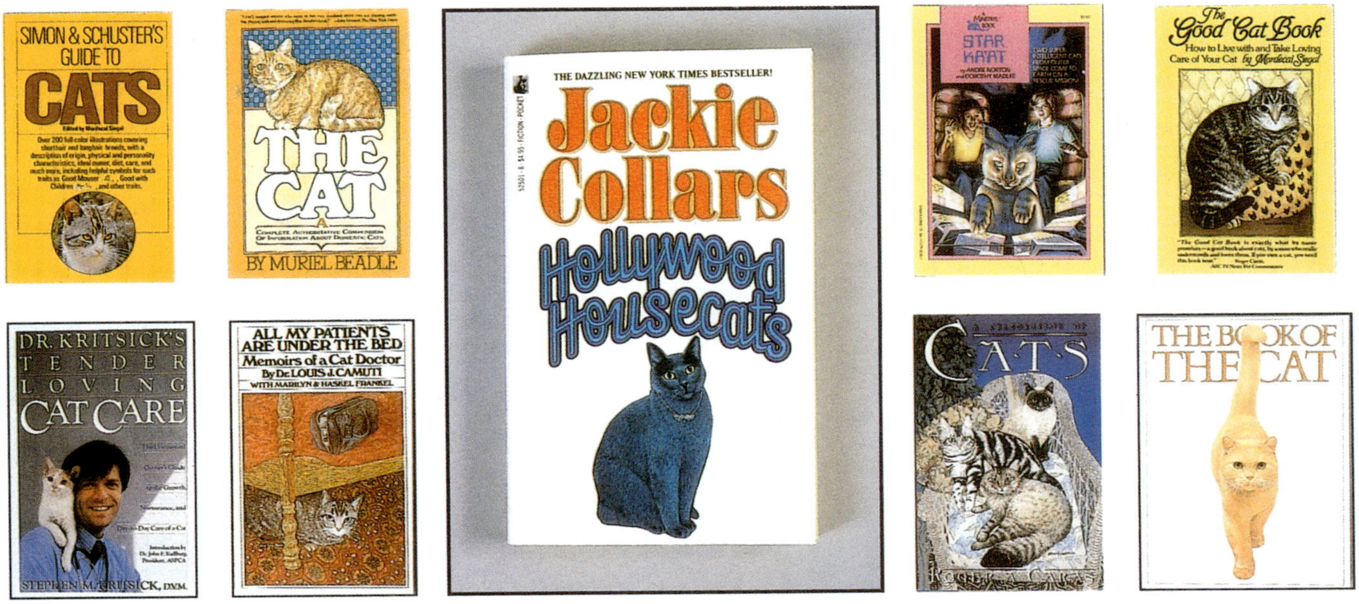

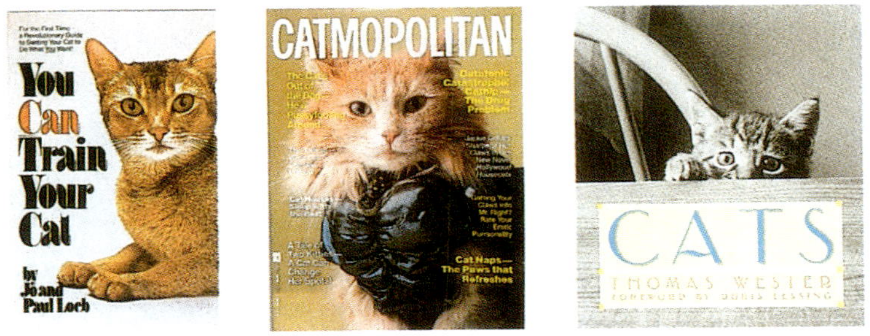

Take 4 for $1
or...Take 3 for 49¢ each

You need only buy all these books in your first month of membership to enable you to receive our weekly catalog of newly published cat books.

Here's how The Litter-ary Guild works: you choose from 2 easy membership plans that fit your purrsonal reading habits.
Choose Plan #1 and after your membership is approved, you get 4 books for only $1. Just buy 4 more books every week for a year, after which you may cancel at any time.
Choose Plan #2 and after your membership is approved you get 3 books for 49¢ each. You may cancel your membership after 6 months, after buying only one book a week.
Relaxed shopping and convenience—collect a cat library in no time!
Buy only the books you want, only the books we offer. New cat books are being published daily, and we want you to see them all!
Plus—our Exclusive Bonus Plan—buy *all* our cat selections, up to 12 titles a week, and we'll throw in a bag of kitty litter for your free membership litter box!

The Litter-ary Guild

PLAN #1	PLAN #2
	FREE Litter Box
FREE Litter Box	

☐ **Plan #1**

☐ **Plan #2**

Name______________________________

Address______________________ Apt.________

City__________ State__________ Zip________

Telephone #________________________

CATMO • HOROSCOPE

by Star Sphynx

Pisces (Feb. 20 • March 20) Always a charitable cat, you will spend time this month collecting funds for one of your pet causes. A friend will ask you for a loan; do it only if you view it as a gift. She'll never give the mousey back! Conflicts between your purrsonal and professional lives pop up on the 10th, 12th, 17th, and 25th. You may have the urge to bury your problems, but your litter box is not a good place for this. Think them through to a solution before they tie you up in a tangled ball.

Aries (March 21 • April 20) This is your chance to succeed! Opportunities to promote your career (whether it be pet therapist or exterminator, food tester or professional escort) are abundant—seize the moment and pounce on it! This is also a time for change. Mars, your ruling planet, has given you the drive to explore new options. It's time to do some housecleaning, both mental and physical. So discard the memory of your summer romance with that elusive tomcat; throw away the ratty catnip mouse he gave you. It's time!

Taurus (April 21 • May 21) The sign of the bull is yours, and you have never been so stubborn! You hold your ground and refuse to listen to others' opinions. This month your persistence pays off, and you are rewarded with a wealth of riches. (The basement *was* filled with mice, and you've caught every one!) Generous Taurean cats will share this bounty with friends, selecting the choicest morsels for that special tomcat. (You weren't born under the influence of Venus without some of her charms rubbing off....)

Gemini (May 22 • June 21) Paired-off twins are ready to call it quits with life-à-deux. You've had it with that tomcat's philandering ways, and Gemini cats deserve better. The influence of Mercury makes you ready to change at a moment's notice—and the time is now! Slip out the window and make tracks for the other side of town. Expand your horizons—you'll never know what you might find. A new romance may await you at the end of your journey....

Cancer (June 22 • July 23) Your docile nature is being tested. Someone has rubbed your fur the wrong way, and you're bristling. Tempers will flare on the 17th; be sure to stand your ground for what you believe in. Others will respect your honesty and determination. Be careful during the full moon on the 23rd. Lunar babies like yourself are especially emotional when the moon shines brightly. Prowl and howl by moonlight, but avoid flying shoes!

Leo (July 24 • Aug. 23) Leos are lion-hearted—you've heard this sentiment before. But this month's events will help you realize how true it is that your home is your castle. On the 15th, people will try to dislodge you from your home. They may put you in a car and take you to a house with unfamiliar smells. Resist the urge to run away and return to your old home. It is wise to spend your time seasoning the new house with *your* smell. Before long, with special attention to the draperies and upholstery, you'll have it looking, and smelling, just like home!

Virgo (Aug. 24 • Sept. 23) Your career has been on hold long enough. It's time to show the world you mean business. Virgo cats should scratch and claw their way to the top, if necessary. They don't call you a "business animal" for nothing! Expose your claws to ward off a catfight on the 10th. By the 19th, your battle will be won and you should be purring with contentment. You're the Top Cat, and you've earned it.

Libra (Sept. 24 • Oct. 23) Until the 12th, ruling planet Venus brings out your seductive nature. The time is right to begin several new love affairs. The Libra cat has her lusty side and this month you can turn up your libido and try as many new tomcats as you can find! (Some resourceful CATMO Cats have been known to line up quite a few suitors....) The scales of justice are your symbol. Remember "an eye for an eye, a tooth for a tooth"? After a weekend of wanton lovemaking, you should begin to prepare for some extra quests in about nine weeks....

Scorpio (Oct. 24 • Nov. 22) You were born under the influence of Pluto (the *planet*, not the *dog*). Scorpio cats exhibit a highly intuitive nature, almost like ESP. Your ancestors may have been burned as witches, but today's Scorpios use their powers wisely to sense danger and other obstacles. Tune in this month. The 4th is a day for subtle changes that set the stage for high drama on the 12th. Follow your instincts and you'll land on your feet. By the 18th, all questions will be resolved and things will settle back into a comfortable routine.

Sagittarius (Nov. 23 • Dec. 21) Jupiter cats should spend time understanding the needs of roommates. Your happy, carefree existence has been sustained at a cost to others, and you may soon have to pay the price for neglecting *their* feelings. Your home is the center of activity, but it must be *shared* (especially if others pay the rent and buy the food). It's exaspurrating to have to compromise your comfort for the sake of theirs, but this is the small price we pay for our daily meals. Patch up the rift with your people (and hide the one on the sofa). Things will be purring along by the end of the month.

Capricorn (Dec. 22 • Jan. 20) Someone has certainly got your goat this month! The influence of Saturn makes you moodier than usual. Your frustrations may vent themselves in destructive ways—curtains, look out! Don't let it happen. Keep your anger under control; it will pass by the 22nd. If you do resort to lashing out at your problems, don't be surprised if you find yourself at the veterinarian's for a dread operation by month's end....Don't say you haven't been warned!

Aquarius (Jan. 21 • Feb. 19) Our water baby is quite a paradox. Yours is an *air* sign and your spirit floats free as the wind. Now is the time to remain steadfast and complete all the projects you have started. (Remember that sweater at the bottom of your basket? You have a sleeve to work on before it is fully unraveled!) Concentrate on creative solutions and success will be yours. The 28th is your special day. By then your work will catapult you to the top, where you'll remain, a paw raised high in victory.

ESPURRIT

Spot
Espurrit Customer and Professional Companion
Age: 7

Sometimes I look out the window and I want to catapult myself into the trees. Oh, to fly! It would make catching birds so much easier. But my family doesn't understand my wild streak. They think I'm tame and obedient. Maybe I am....Maybe that's why they gave me this strange name. Spot. Like a pet dog. It couldn't possibly have anything to do with the markings on my head. They're not spots, they're beauty marks.

YOUR BIG ODD EYES MAY NEVER BE THE SAME AGAIN.

Presenting Cat's Eyes, the first contact lenses that can change the darkest odd eyes to bright, matched colors.

Go from brown to blue in a flash. Change a blue eye to green for a matched set!

While odd-eyed cats previously had to endure the scrutinizing stares of cats with matching eyes, Cat's Eyes lenses let you change the color of one eye to match the other. Or change the color of both eyes to an exciting new color.

The results can be amazing. A new eye color can highlight your best features, your facial fur, make a visible difference in the way you look.

Best of all, the lenses are brightly colored, so they won't get lost if they fall into your water dish. And Cat's Eyes may be worn all day and night, to enhance your beauty during late-night travels.

So see your veterinarian to obtain a correct and comfortable fit.

Tomorrow your eyes may be the beautiful colors you've always wanted.

Cat's Eyes Lenses

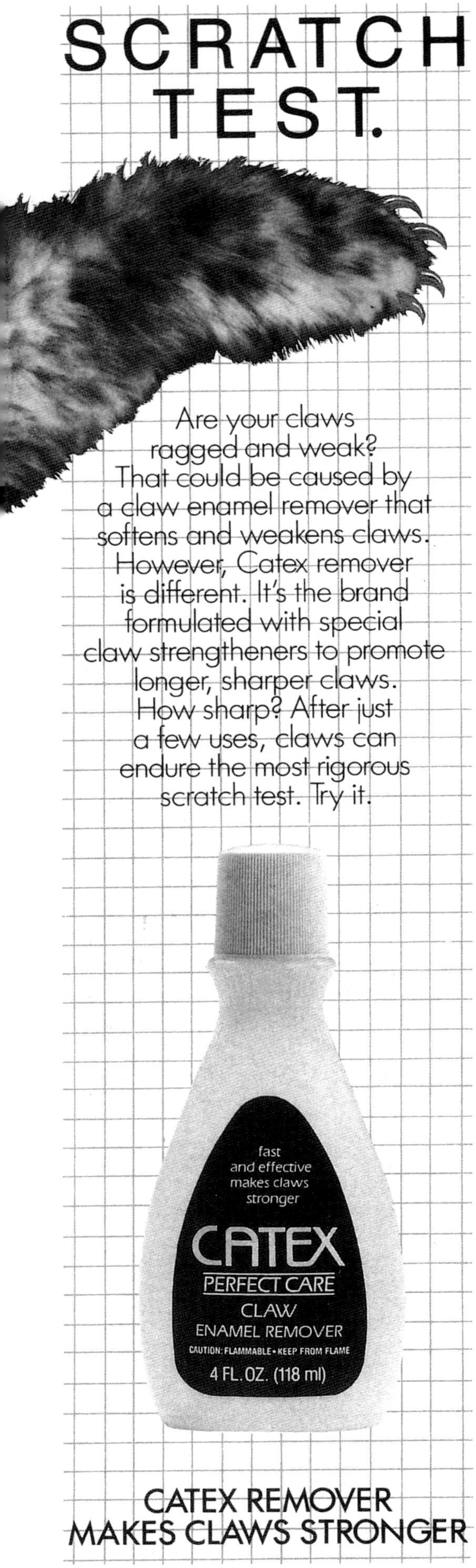

HEALTH memo:

News from the Veterinary World

the swab rolls in on little cat teeth....

Cats who eat little dry food (and I have a feeling that this includes *most* of you) may begin to notice a deposit on your teeth. In time, tooth decay and gum disease may begin. Not to mention the crimp that bad breath will put in your active social life... *Cat-O-Dontics* are specially treated tooth-cleaning pads. They're easy to use—just enlist your person. The pad is wrapped around a cotton swab, and is then wiped over your teeth. Do not bite your person's hand while she is doing this or she will be reluctant to help you out again....

CDH
3803 Mariana Way
Santa Barbara, CA 93105
(805) 682-5717

fur will fly...out!

Your daily grooming ritual can have a dangerous side effect—hairballs. Long-haired cats are particularly susceptible to this painful condition. If unchecked, hairballs collect in the digestive tract, causing constipation, lethargy, dry cough, and even spitting up. Not a pretty picture... Daily brushing does help, but the best remedy is one of the easiest. *Petromalt* is a gel that lubricates the intestinal tract to aid in the elimination of hairballs. A small quantity of this tasty gelatin can be licked off your paw or taken straight from the tube. It's definitely a hair-splitting experience!

St. Jon Petcare, Inc.
1656 W. 240th Street
Harbor City, CA 90710
(213) 326-2720

feline first aid

How would you respond to an emergency? Some fraidy cats would grow catatonic with fear. Don't lose precious time. Consult the *First-Aid and Emergency Treatments Slide Chart for Dogs and Cats*. Keep this handy device near your medicine chest or first-aid kit. It could save a life—maybe yours. This simple sliding chart provides instant answers to first-aid questions and is essential to help you respond quickly and correctly to an accident or injury.

Kramer Computer Aids, Inc.
P.O. Box 57
Red Bank, NJ 07701

flea market

Alley cats and show cats can suffer from the same age-old problem—fleas. There are many ways to fight them; we suggest two. Purists and hep cats believe in holistic cures. For these categories, we recommend a natural, herbal flea collar. Two possible varieties are *Nature's Best Herbal Flea Collar* and *Natural Herbal Flea Collar*, both available from Natural Research People, Inc. Both collars are safe and rely on five patented flea-repelling natural oils. The collars differ only in style: the *Nature's Best* collar is made of durable vinyl; the *Natural Herbal Flea Collar* has the same ingredients impregnated into a cord to be tied around your neck (for tomcats it imparts that rugged outdoors look).

Natural Research People, Inc.
South Rt.—Box 12
Lavina, MT 59046
(406) 575-4343

Corpurrate fat cats will relate better to the flea collar with the tech-touch... *The Microtech-2 Flea Collar for Cats*. This small electronic device, attached to a "breakaway" adjustable collar, emits a "Pulse-Modulated Burst Circuit" (PMBC) that creates high-frequency sound heard by fleas and ticks, but not by cats. It's water-resistant, veterinarian-tested, and effective.

Elexis, Corp.
7000 NW 46th Street
Miami, FL 33166
1-800-327-1033

cats on the couch

Cats can suffer from stress and emotional disorders like anyone else. Now we can call upon the feline's Freud to unravel the mysteries of our "Catsonalities." Cat therapist Carole Wilbourn is the author of four books on cat behavior. She also writes a monthly column (called "Cats on the Couch") for *Cat Fancy Magazine*. She has been called "the founding mother of feline psychotherapy." Ms. Wilbourn has treated more than 10,000 cats, and her success rate, as estimated by one veterinarian, is 75 percent. Many problems can be resolved in a single therapy session, although more severe cases may require additional appointments. Ms. Wilbourn is available for consultation and can be contacted at (212) 741-0397. The book *Cats on the Couch: The Complete Guide for Loving and Caring for Your Cat* can be ordered from **The Humane Society of New York, 306 East 59th Street, New York, NY 10022.** All proceeds go to The Humane Society, which published the book.

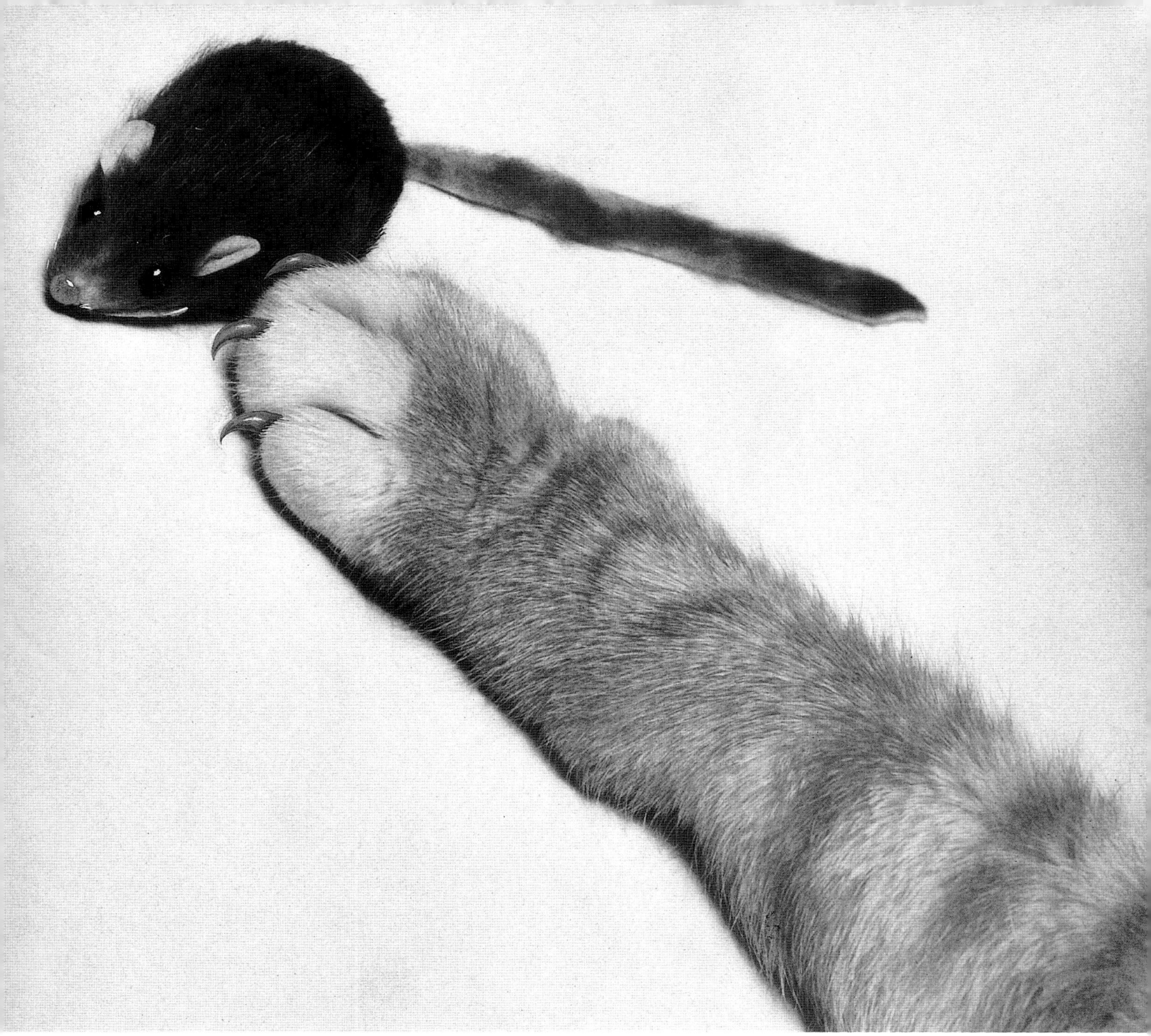

IF YOU WANT STRONG CLAWS, PUT THEM ON A HEALTHY DIET.

A diet for claws that is perfectly balanced for all cats, with nutrients to benefit all of your body. And that's why Siamese Hansen, the claw expert, brings you all the basics you need to become healthier and stronger.

Overnight Claw Treatment restores strength while you sleep. Claw Biter discourages the bad habit while preventing ragged claw tips. Hard as Claws with Nylon provides lasting color and protection for active paws. Hard as Claws strengthens weak claws with regular use. And Caticle Massage Cream softens paws, especially the tender area around your claws.

Naturally, all our products are groomer-tested for scratch resistance. After all, what would you expect from the makers of Hard as Claws?

Siamese Hansen. Because healthy claws are strong claws.

Siamese Hansen®

BEAUTY BEGINS WITH CLAWS.

Photograph by Bruce Plotkin

PAWS TO CATCH YOUR BREATH:

CATHLETICS AND FELINE FITNESS

By Javanese Fonda

□ The Fat Cat used to feel secure in her position. She could point to well-known (and well-fed) cats in the media, like Garfield and Morris, as role models (or was that "roll" models?). Fat cats pulled their weight where it counted. But one day she noticed that the cat calls were no more. Her day in the sun had passed, and slim cats were the new sex kittens. The tide had turned to thin. The catchwords included *trim, lean,* and (heaven forbid) *muscular.* What was a lazy fat cat to do?

No longer could she lie around eating catnip bonbons. Something drastic had to be done! All around her she saw svelte cats in clingy collars, with firm shoulders, abdomens, and thighs. She could never compete for eligible tomcats in the deplorable shape she was in. She would have to slim down, and do it fast, unless she wanted to spend the rest of her life alone, munching on mouseburgers....

Well, fat CATMO Cats, help is on the way, my dears. There's more than one way to trim a cat! This brief guide to the latest developments in Cathletics is sure to have a method that works for *you.*

Intellectual cats will resort to the books in search of the purrfect way to lose weight and firm up. *Reading* diet and exercise books, however, is not enough. You must follow the book's instructions if you want to take off pounds and inches! One good book to consult is called **Pet Aerobics,** by Warren and Faye Eckstein (Henry Holt and Company).

Media kitties, addicted to cat TV, can slim down by exercising along with a tape. One popular exercise tape is **Pet-ercises** from Petcetera. It features routines like four-paw pushups to push you back into shape in a hurry.

Exercise equipment is the newest addition to any feline fitness program. Several companies have designed effective pieces of "machinery" to alleviate the drudgery of exercise. The idea is that if you enjoy the process of exercise when using one of these highly developed pieces of equipment, you are likely to exercise more often (and even joyfully, as evidenced by the happy expression of our model as she samples each "machine").

The House of the Mouse is a skilled routine requiring concentration as well as stamina. **The Amazen Kitty Maze** strengthens all four leg muscles as you bat the ball and dome across the floor. **The Cork Scratching Post** features a catnip-filled ball for additional motivation. **The Catnip Lolly Pop** will provide you with vigorous upper-body workout. **The Catnip-filled Cat Head,** suspended on cord, will inspire you to dance aerobically across a room.

Each piece of equipment has been scientifically designed to induce a basically lazy cat to utilize the machine to her fullest benefit. This is done by introducing catnip, a natural stimulant, into the design of each exercise aid. You'll be drawn to the equipment, and you'll use it often—you'll be reluctant to relinquish your machine to another cat! You'll be slim, trim, and beautiful in no time, once you get the tiger by the tail. Don't give up until your cat walk inspires cat calls again!

The Catnip-filled Cat Head

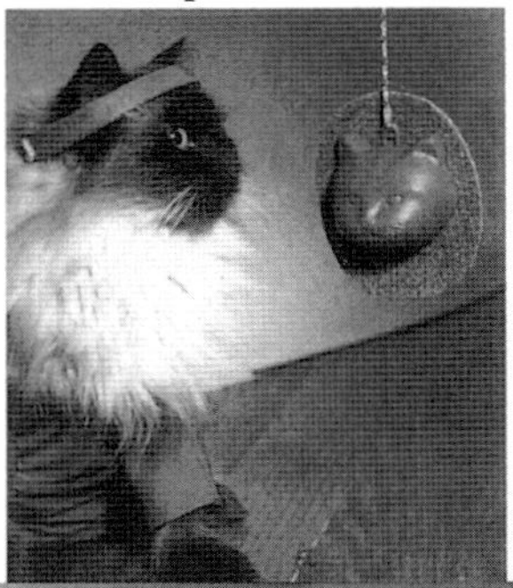

The Cork Scratching Post

The Catnip Lolly Pop

The House of the Mouse

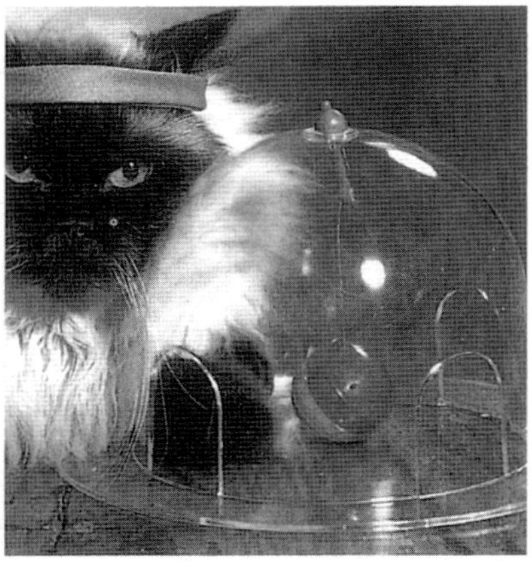

The Amazen Kitty Maze

Where to purrchase on last page.

The International Cat Games are a proposed Olympics for the feline set. The events have been designed to highlight the cat's best cathletic accomplishments. Tryouts have been postponed, however, because the contestants were too lazy to leave their homes to compete. Until new tryouts can be rescheduled, you will have to be content with the set of posters that was especially designed to commemorate this auspicious event.

GARFIELD

The Ultimate Entrepreneur

In ten short years, he's taken the corpurrate world by storm.

By Japanese Bobtail Davis

☐ He's fat and lazy, with a grumpy disposition. Yet, in spite of these qualities (or, as he prefers to think, because of them), Garfield has catapulted to the top of the corpurrate battlefield. This formidable feline has engineered a remarkable expansion, from the star of newspaper comic strips (from 40 papers to over 1,900 in just ten years), into a myriad of fascinating and lucrative business ventures.

Indeed, since the Garfield comic strip first appeared in 1978, Garfield has become one of the most famous and best-loved cats in history. Every day millions of fans around the world read his syndicated comic strip. It appears in 37 countries, in 12 different languages, and is one of the world's most popular comic strips, second only to *Peanuts* (which features a *dog*, of all things!). In America, however, Garfield is *the* most popular comic strip, recognized and preferred by more than 75% of adults, 93% of teens, and 96% of children, as discovered in an independent study conducted in 1986.

Garfield, never one to rest on his laurels (although he does seem to rest on everything else), decided to use his popularity and business acumen to develop a number of businesses. A creative cat, and most adept at writing, he first explored the world of publishing. A contract with Ballantine Books has been beneficial to both parties. He has published 22 trade paperback books to date, and each one has appeared on *The New York Times* Best-Seller List. In fact, Garfield enjoys the rare distinction of having 7 books appear on the list *simultaneously*. (Look out, Jackie Collars!)

The best-selling author followed a traditional route from writing into acting. The television public, captivated with his sparkling purrsonality during numerous media appearances to promote his books, demanded to see more of the star in the fur. This led to the production of five prime-time animated Garfield specials. In his inimitable manner, Garfield once again took the industry by storm, and all five programs were nominated for Emmy Awards. Garfield won the coveted award for Outstanding Animated Program for three consecutive years, in 1983, 1984, and 1985. In 1985, the winner, "Garfield's Halloween Adventure," was up against some very strong competition, "Garfield in Paradise." No wonder the top cat emerged victorious once again!

All five television programs received top Nielsen ratings, so Garfield has gone back to the studio to produce two more specials, to be aired in late 1987.

Once again, as success bred success, Garfield was led into yet another related business. He was urged to make purrsonal appearances. His great love for the public, combined with his innate hamminess, had convinced him that he would be well received. The response was overwhelming. "The Garfield Magic Show" has had over 2,000 performances since its opening in 1983, and it's still going strong. The show is a great favorite wherever it is performed, especially in shopping malls and city centers. The popularity of the magic show inspired a new theatrical production, "Garfield's Furry Tales," in successful road productions across America.

In addition to these two theatrical productions, Garfield continues to make purrsonal appearances, whether to help a retailer promote a Garfield line of products (more about this later), or to support one of his pet causes. Garfield enjoys his special visits to children's hospitals, and he always travels to Washington for Easter to participate in the Annual Easter Egg Roll on the White House lawn.

Like many other famous purrsonalities, Garfield chose to capitalize on his name through entry into the field of licensing. He works with more than 300 companies to develop and market more than 3,000 Garfield products that are sold here and abroad.

Garfield takes special pride in these ventures, and he and his staff devote a lot of time and effort to create products that are both attractive and functional. They also conform to the highest levels of quality, as Garfield stipulates that all of his licensees be leaders in their fields of business. Garfield products range from underwear to plush toys to stationery items, with new businesses constantly approaching the multitalented cat.

In a related business move, Garfield began to offer his services as a spokescat to a variety of successful corporations. He has produced promotional items for a cereal company, filmed television commercials for a chain of hotels, and even appeared on billboards to publicize a real estate venture. Perhaps his finest moment was during an American Express "Do you know me?" commercial, when in an unprecedented event, they *did* know him, even before examining his credit card!

Many have questioned why this cat is so well loved and so successful. The commonly upheld image of a ruthless business-cat clawing his way to the top does not conform to the Garfield we have seen here. To what does he owe his popularity? One explanation, offered by Garfield's friend and companion, Jim Davis, is simple:

"We live in a time when we're made to feel guilty about overeating, oversleeping, not exercising; and Garfield militantly defends his right to do all of those things, thereby relieving some of our guilt. He has the courage of his convictions to say and do a lot of things a lot of us would like to, but don't."

This quality, combined with the business savvy of a true professional, has made Garfield the top cat in publishing, broadcasting, marketing, and promotion. Garfield is truly the cat with clout.

COPYCATS— PUSSY PAWTRAITURE

Cats have long fascinated artists, who have tried to capture our grace and mystery in a variety of media. A visit to a local museum, or a glance through an art book like ***Metropolitan Cats*** *(published by Harry N. Abrams), should be enough to convince you that people artists have often been successful in their efforts. Several of the contemporary artists caught by our animal magnetism show examples of their work here.*

Mimi Vang Olsen is known as "The Pet Portrait Painter." You have probably seen her work in books, magazines, and on gift items. She is best known for her sensitive and purrceptive oil paintings, like the one seen here, or in the illustrations for pages 50 and 91 of this magazine.

Gloria Vanderbilt shows her good breeding in her lithograph of "Oyster Cat," a real aristocat! This lithograph is available through The Margo Feiden Galleries.

Gino Beghe has painted "Bartender Cat," and lithographs of the painting are available from The Margo Feiden Galleries. ("I'll have a dish of cream, straight up. . . .") He also created the painting of the cat at the fish store seen on page 96.

Wynne Gilmore designs beautiful silk garments hand-painted with vivid images. The silk scarf shown here is one of the original designs that can be commissioned to pawtray yourself and your friends in your natural habitat. The silk can also be made up into cushions or garments—the choice is yours.

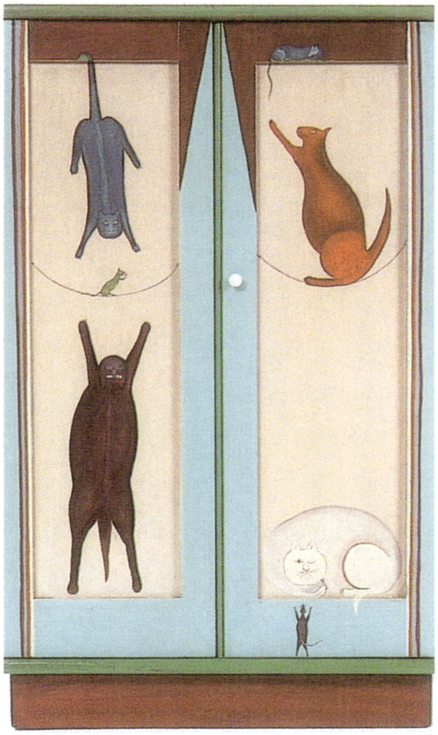

Friedrich Gross applies his art to a variety of surfaces—canvas, furniture, and even the facades of buildings! The cupboard shown here is a whimsical look at good mousekeeping!

Thaddeus Krumeich incorporates cats into trompe l'oeil subjects. His paintings are reminiscent of the primitive efforts of early American artists. Most of his works are 3-dimensional and incorporate their own frame—a "cat box" of sorts!

Susan Gray has devised a way for people to keep their favorite cat (you) close to their hearts. She designed a 22K brooch or pendant that frames your hand-painted miniature pawtrait. Done with tiny sable brushes (you deserve the best), and with the frame finished with a baroque pearl drop, the pawtraits are pretty pricey. But you're worth it!

Laura Dabrowski creates whimsical fur-niture adorned with cat likenesses. Her collection includes chairs for both children and adults, tables, and decorative items like her "corner cats," wall murals, and shirts embellished with fanciful felines.

Jeff Tritel creates a sculpture that "hops" with kittenish glee. "Hopscotch Kitty" is cast in bronze and shows a young cat just kitten around!

Robert Guzman-Forbes creates custom cat pawtraits by commission in pastel, watercolor, prismapencil, or acrylic paints. The resulting works show a sensitive understanding of feline nature.

Al Hirschfeld immortalizes famous personalities in his inimitable style. Now he will do the same for "Purrsonalities"! He can be commissioned for pawtraits like the one shown here (of the late Marlin Perkins and a feline friend) through The Margo Feiden Galleries.

Victoria Nodiff calls this work "Cat" (we can't imagine why!). Of monumental proportions, this multimedia work (a collage of gouache, acrylic, glitter, and book page) pawtrays the cat as larger than life.

Jim and Ann Monteith of The Monteith Studio & Gallery are two of the premier photographers of pet pawtraiture. They can capture you in a familiar setting or create a feline fantasy.

Julie Evans paints miniature cat pawtraits and frames them in antique frames from her extensive collection. The resulting little gems can adorn a desk or tabletop or be hung on a wall to make a small but elegant statement. Sometimes smaller is more beautiful. . . .

Where to purrchase on last page.

Pussies galore:

FELINE FIGURINES AND CAT COLLECTIBLES

People have a penchant for collecting cat creations—figurines of felines and other pussy products are particularly popular. They have even formed an organization to commemorate and celebrate cat collections! Cat Collectors is a club whose members enjoy the common interest of collecting cat figurines, books, artwork, advertisements, calendars, postcards, paper products, needlework, jewelry, antiques, bottles, teapots, and other items bearing a cat motif. The group puts out a bimonthly illustrated newsletter and catalogue. They can be contacted at 31311 Blair Drive, Warren, MI 48092, (313) 264-0285.

Tyber Katz© are a labor of love produced by Peter and Pat Tyber. Peter carves the heads and paws by hand from Oregon pine. Pat paints the heads and paws, adding whiskers of genuine horsehair. The bodies are created from kid or muslin, and each cat is outfitted with a fully detailed costume made from silk and other fine fabrics. The cats are signed and numbered, as each one is unique and part of a limited-edition design. The group pictured here is "Les Chats Tyber," available in an edition of 350.

Fitz and Floyd has provided us with this "mug shot"—Toby mug. This mug, called "Hey Diddle Diddle, Cat with a Fiddle," is part of a set which also includes a pitcher. Pitcher and mug are sold separately.

Marjory Warren works wonders with bits of fabric. Her appliqué designs of cats adorn cushions and clothing items. Steal a cushion from the sofa—it makes a great bed!

Authentic Models Holland has created a charming group of traditional nesting dolls. Each of the four hand-painted cats conceals a secret: either a smaller cat or, in the smallest cat, a mouse. They are fun as playthings, small boxes, or as displays of decorative objects.

"The Curio Cabinet Cats" are available exclusively from The Franklin Mint. The eclectic group of 15 cat sculptures represents the art style of a particular country or period from American Folk Art to Art Nouveau. They are crafted from a diverse group of materials—from chalkwear to porcelain to pewter. The collection is displayed in a handsome glass-and-brass vitrine.

Daniel Brooks has produced a unique table base of Egyptian cats. Cast in bronze, it is a beautiful addition to any decor—your people will love it.

B. Shackman & Co. has designed a full line of collectibles that features its favorite feline, *Kitty Cucumber*. The range of products is vast, from paper goods to porcelain figurines and music boxes, among many others. A selection of products from the line is shown here.

Adorables are charming miniature figures that pawtray pussies in a warm and whimsical manner. The figurines are hand-painted and are imported from Scotland by Private Showing.

Loeber Cats are examples of fiber arts—hand-woven textile sculpture in brushed wools and mohairs. The facial features of these catlike creatures are embroidered with 3-dimensional trapunto detail. They are further enhanced with paint that is delicately applied to blend the hair into the faces. Loeber Cats are cushionlike forms, while "Pussykins," like those illustrated here, are a delightful amalgam of cats and people, fully dressed in romantic, nostalgic costumes.

Barbara Gallup of **Totally Topiary** has designed an unusual pair of Cat Topiaries especially for CATMO. She can create a custom design for you of plant materials that will need watering or of dried moss, as in the pair shown, which require no care. Some recent commissions have included birds, but mice are also possible!

Where to purrchase on last page.

Getting Your Claws into Mr Right?

Rate Your Erotic Purrsonality

By Raquel Rex

□ Female felines are known for their sensuous and seductive ways. But cats can fall into three different categories of sexual behavior—the uninhibited Wildcat, the romantic Pussycat, and the nurturing Housecat. These three purrsonality types give off distinct signals to tomcats; they are signals that can be easily read—or misread.

Are you a Wildcat, Pussycat, or Housecat? Your mode of behavior may be purrceived as you have intended, or you may be purrplexing your tomcat with crossed signals. You may be hunting for a top cat and find yourself with an alleycat instead!

Find out which of the three purrsonality types is closest to your own, and the type of tomcat who is attracted to each. You may be surprised at the results of the quiz, but your answers will help provide you with a plan to give off the *right* kind of signals from now on to attract your own "Mr. Right"! So, sharpen your claws and begin...

QUIZ

1. Your sexual fantasy would be:

a. Curling up together on a cozy windowsill, listening to the sound of the rain.

b. A simple and successful mating that would produce a litter of healthy kittens.

c. A heat that never ends! Wild sex with as many tomcats as I can find!

2. Can you handle sexual relationships with two tomcats at the same time?

a. I would find it hard to cheat on my mate, and I would be crushed if he did it to me.

b. Only *two*? I usually juggle *several* suitors at once!

c. Only if I were in love with *both* of them—sex without love is meaningless.

3. What would you most like to receive as a love offering?

a. A naughty red satin catnip mouse.

b. A bouquet of freshly picked catnip.

c. A shiny new litter box with disposable liner bags.

4. How would you describe your past relationships?

a. Strong and handsome tomcats who prowl the neighborhood have always caught my eye.

b. I mated with the tomcat who lived next door. We had known each other since we were kittens.

c. A quick roll in the hay, and then I can't remember their names or faces.

5. What do you look for in a tomcat?

a. A reliable and mature tomcat who'd make a good father.

b. Good looks and sexual purrformance—I like the strong silent type.

c. A handsome but sensitive tomcat with a sense of humor.

6. How do you feel at the start of an affair?

a. Excited and anxious to have more.

b. Tingly. I love the early stages of a romance.

c. I add his name to mine and dream about what our kittens would look like.

7. Where do you prefer to make love?

a. I like to curl up amid lacy pillows on the bed.

b. My own backyard is a safe and comfortable place for mating.

c. Anyplace will do, as long as it's good and often.

8. How well must you know a tomcat before you make love with him?

a. I am not attracted to strangers. I have to know the tomcat, and his family, *well*.

b. I'll try any tomcat who answers my call. "Try it, you'll like it" is my motto.

c. I like to know the tomcats I mate with. An afternoon together in the yard is the prelude to romance.

9. What is your favorite movie?

a. *Fritz the Cat*

b. *The Owl and the Pussycat*

c. *That Darn Cat*

10. How do you feel about one-night stands?

a. I don't believe in making them a habit, but occasionally I am swept off my paws. . . .

b. I find them morally wrong. If *we* can't set a good example for our kittens, who will?

c. Great! How many can I fit into a week?!!

Scoring

	a.	b.	c.
1.	P	H	W
2.	H	W	P
3.	W	P	H
4.	P	H	W
5.	H	W	P
6.	W	P	H
7.	P	H	W
8.	H	W	P
9.	W	P	H
10.	P	H	W

The letter you circled most often reveals your erotic purrsonality type: H for Housecat, P for Pussycat, and W for Wildcat. If your choices are evenly divided between two or more of the groups, you have purrsonality traits of each. Read below for a description of your erotic purrsonality.

Housecat: You believe in the traditional values of home and family. Nothing pleases you more than a warm litter of kittens suckling at your breasts. Mating is a necessary evil to achieve this goal, so mate you must. Don't be put off by the sharp pain you associate with sex. It is the small price you must pay to create a healthy litter of kittens. Your ideal mate is a mature and dependable housecat; often he's the cat next door. He is sure to stick around for the birth of your kittens. But once they're weaned, he's usually gone and the responsibility for raising them is left to you. You hardly mind, however. What else are mothers for?

Pussycat: You are a cute,cuddly ball of fur. A hopeless romantic, you dream of the day when your tomcat will come. You've learned the game of cat and mouse, and have even earned a reputation as a tom-teaser. Nice cats *do,* so you would be wise to act upon your attractions now and then. Don't pussyfoot around—if you spot an attractive tomcat, go for it. Exude your animal magnetism (if you've got it, flaunt it!) and go in for the kill! Be assertive in the purrsuit of your tomcat. There's no use crying over spilt milk—if he's not the one for you, try again with someone new!

Wildcat: You're the cat's meow, and you *know* it. Your seductive cat walk is met by cat calls from one and all. *Every* tomcat is your prey. From the alleycat to the housecat, you want to meet, and mate with, them all! Your modus operandi is to lure them back to your lion's den for some real fun. No scaredy cat, you. You look just like the cat that ate the canary! A leopard can't change her spots—you're a tigress in the bedroom. You leave your lovers as weak as kittens, while you emerge gratified and fulfilled, grinning from ear to ear like a Cheshire cat. One look at a tomcat brings out the animal in you. You are happy with your sexual smorgasbord, and your cathouse behavior will ensure a constant supply of tomcats at your door. It's raining cats—and you're in the catbird seat!

Be a cagey cat—lure him into your lion's den with a romantic meal for two that will unleash his emotions. A selection of pâtés is served with home-baked biscuits. The dried food adds a delightful change of texture. Serve with dishes of your favorite light, white drink (water). Pussy willows and cattails make a charming centerpiece, while your selection of china reveals your simple elegance and good breeding. Now, just curl up together, and enjoy the evening....

(SEE PAGE 22 FOR COOKBOOKS AND CAT FOODS.)

FOOD EDITOR: PAT SCOTTISH FOLD
PHOTOGRAPHS BY: BRUCE PLOTKIN

CAT SUP

Where to purrchase on last page.

CATMO·TALKS·TO MORRIS THE CAT

AMERICA'S MOST FAMOUS FELINE PURRSONALITY

This media mogul is the picture of success. Everything he touches turns to gold. He's given a helping paw to a variety of pet causes. Where will he leave his paw print next?

By Tabby Thompson

□ Morris is the most famous feline media figure in America. Like other well-known purrsonalities—Cher, Barbra, Mick, Brooke, Oprah, and Garfield, to name only a few—Morris needs just one name to identify him. The mention of that single name, Morris, immediately calls to mind the handsome and popular tomcat who makes frequent appearances on behalf of his favorite causes. Turn on your TV; you're certain to see him promoting his pet product on a program to benefit public health or the homeless. Visit a cat show; chances are that he, or a representative of his corporation, is there to bestow the coveted Morris Award upon another worthy mixed-breed cat. But what's next for this famous feline?

We recently had the opportunity to speak with Morris and his human companion, Bob Martwick. Bob is sometimes erroneously referred to as Morris's trainer, when in fact it is *Bob* who has been trained by *Morris* to look after our favorite cat's every whim and need! Morris prefers to think of Bob as his valet.

CATMO met with Morris at his luxurious home in the Chicago area. There we talked to both Morris and Bob to uncover some new facets of Morris's purrsonality. Bob's answers are indicated by the letter B, and Morris's thoughts by the letter M. Their replies were quite candid—we're sure you'll be pleased and surprised to discover new things about your favorite tomcat!

Q. How old is Morris?
B. About 8. His exact birth date is unknown, as is his parentage, because he was adopted from a shelter.
M. "We stars always lie about our age anyway."
Q. Where was he born?
B. Somewhere on the East Coast. Morris was just a simple stray wandering the streets before he landed in an animal shelter.
M. "9-Lives adopted me, and the rest is history."
Q. What breed is he?
B. Alleycat...mixed breed...often called domestic shorthair.
M. "Let's not get fancy about it."
Q. How did Morris become the spokescat for 9-Lives?
B. He met all the qualifications—big, orange-striped, finicky, and photogenic.
M. "My animal magnetism took me from straydom to stardom."
Q. Where does Morris live?
B. He lives with me in west suburban Chicago.
M. "Bob is my valet."
Q. What does Morris's bachelor pad look like?
M. "Depends on whether it's the maid's day off."
B. We live in an average-size home with a large yard. Morris sleeps in a simple cardboard box underneath my desk.
Q. How does he spend a typical day?
B. He acts like a normal cat—stalking around, teasing the dogs, and watching TV.
M. "I prefer watching 9-Lives commercials."
Q. How much does Morris travel for business?
B. About three months out of the year.
M. "First class, of course."
Q. What television appearances has Morris made?
B. Morris has appeared on "Lifestyles of the Rich and Famous"; "Entertainment Tonight"; "Good Morning America"; "The Today Show"; "CBS Morning Program"; "The Merv Griffin Show"; "Hour Magazine"; "CNN Showbiz Today"; "PM Magazine"; "Foul-ups, Bleeps and Blunders."
M. "This list goes on and on."
Q. What awards has Morris won?
B. The Patsy Award for the best animal actor in TV commercials. Morris was also voted "Most Admired Male" by *Young Miss* magazine readers, and "Animal Star of the Year" by readers of *Us* magazine three years in a row. Cat Health Month, which featured Morris, received the "Gentle Doctor" and "Golden Key" awards from the veterinary profession.
M. "Today the Patsy, tomorrow the universe."
Q. What are Morris's favorite causes and charities?
B. Morris's pet causes include Adopt-a-Cat Month, Cat Health Month, and the National Morris Award. Morris is official spokescat for all three.
M. "I'm quite the philanthrocat."
Q. Tell us about the National Morris Award.
B. The Morris Award was created to honor beauty and excellence in mixed breeds, like Morris. It is given to the Best Household Pet at more than 400 cat shows every year. Local winners can then compete for a national title to name the best mixed-breed cat in the country. The first National Morris Award was held at The Cat Club in New York. 9-Lives flew in the 12 finalists from all over the country. There was great fanfare—cat dancers, limos, celebrity judges JoAnne Worley, Veronica Hamel, Earl Holliman, and others. The event benefited Actors and Others for Animals. The winner, Miami Vice, got a giant trophy and a year's supply of 9-Lives Cat Food.
M. "Everyone wants a Morris."
Q. Tell us about Adopt-a-Cat Month.
B. Adopt-a-Cat Month is a June campaign sponsored by 9-Lives for the American Humane Association and more than 800 participating animal shelters. It promotes the adoption of cats and kittens from shelters. It also helps educate the public about the importance of spaying and neutering to prevent cat overpopulation. Adopt-a-Cat Month has helped more than a million cats find homes since it began in 1974.
M. "The simple pleasures...a happy home, loving owner, and 9-Lives for din-din."
Q. Tell us about Cat Health Month.
B. This campaign is designed to educate cat owners to their pet's need for regular veterinary care. Less than half of cat owners take their cats in for check-ups and vaccinations, compared to 74 percent of dog owners. 9-Lives launched a September campaign called Cat Health Month. Morris and I went on the road with his consulting veterinarian, Dr. Laura Pasten,

to spread this critical message nationwide.
M. "I'm always on call for good health."
Q. What booklets and articles has Morris written?
B. With the help of some friends at 9-Lives, he's authored "Morris: An Intimate Biography"; "The Morris Approach: An Insider's Guide to Cat Care"; "The Morris Method: A Guide to Cat Care"; and "℞ The Morris Prescription: A Guide to Cat Health Care."
M. "I'm multitalented."
Q. What is his favorite food?
B. 9-Lives Canned Gourmet, 9-Lives Crunchy Meals, and 9-Lives Tender Meals. Super Supper is Morris's favorite flavor.
M. "So many flavors, so little time."
Q. What are Morris's hobbies?
B. Watching TV commercials, being finicky, eating din-din.
M. "9-Lives, of course."
Q. What are his pet peeves?
B. People who play with his tail.
M. "Humans can be so annoying."
Q. What is Morris's astrological sign?
B. Probably a Leo.
M. "The only stars I watch are on the screen."
Q. What does Morris look for in a female cat?
B. Knowing Morris, he probably looks for feline intelligence, animal magnetism, impeccable taste, and catty charm.
M. "I'm very selective."
Q. What does Morris's ideal female look like?
B. Tabby fur, long legs, a high arch, inquisitive eyes, and soft whiskers.
M. "Right out of the 'purrsonal' ads."
Q. What would Morris do on a dream date?
B. Probably take her for a cruise in a limo and find a romantic spot in a back alley for a little 9-Lives din-din on a silver platter.
M. "Only the best!"
Q. Is he seeing anyone special right now?
B. No, he's too busy with purrsonal appearances, photo sessions, and travel.
M. "That doesn't mean I don't read the menu."
Q. What are Morris's plans for the future?
B. More of the same... commercials, calendars, purrsonal appearances, etc.
M. "Fame is the name of the game."
Q. How would he like to be remembered?
B. He's not planning on leaving real soon.
M. "Legends live on forever."
Q. Does Morris have any regrets?
B. I don't think so.
M. "Giving Bob Martwick control of the can opener."
Q. If he could live his life over again, what would Morris do differently?
B. He'd probably run for President or write another book.
M. "I'd call it *The Nine Lives and Finicky Times of Morris the Cat.*"
Q. Does Morris have a favorite motto or slogan?
B. You can never be too rich or too finicky.
M. "Finickiness is next to godliness."
Q. Who is the most interesting person he has met or known?
M. "Besides myself?"
B. Morris thinks JoAnne Worley is a pretty neat gal. She was the emcee for his first National Morris Award.
Q. If Morris could have one wish come true, what would it be?
B. He would wish for every cat in America to have a happy home and a loving owner.
M. "And din-din on demand."
Q. Who does Morris most admire?
B. Besides himself? In all modesty, probably me. I'm his valet, handler, and, most important, the hand that feeds.
M. "Humility has its rewards."
Q. If he could live in any time, when would Morris choose?
B. The present. Cats are now the number one pet, a well-deserved and much-enjoyed status. They're living up to the true meaning of the word *domestic*. Morris, of course, influenced cats' popularity.
M. "One giant step for catkind."

CAT TRAVEL UPDATE

[continued from 26]

ties. But the special touch that keeps customers coming back is their lovely shop, which carries a complete selection of accessories for cats, as well as items featuring a cat motif. These make wonderful gifts for your people. We know how you like to buy them a little something when you return from a trip, to provide those family members left behind with a bit of the fun you experienced. The cat-oriented gifts sold here will certainly fill the bill and will bring pleasure into the lives of the people back home. The Cat's Pajamas can be visited at 10928 Westheimer, Suite A, Houston, TX 77042, (713) 952-CATS.

Travel Away in a Kitty Car

Cats on the go are always on the lookout for the best limousine services. (You know, darling, to take you to the groomer, to lunch, and then to a brief stop at the vet before heading off to the airport for a trip to the Coast.) Bi-coastal kitties know the numbers to call to assure the best service in New York and L.A. In New York, clever cats call (718) 377-2929. That's the number for the Critter Car, an exclusive taxi service for *all* animals (so you can bring your pet mouse along for the ride). In L.A., cats in the know call (213) 651-LIMO. That number will connect you with Pet Limo, which offers a similar service in the Los Angeles area. Cats on a jaunt to the Continent can call (1) 878-5122 on their arrival in London. This will reach Move-a-Pet, Ltd., which provides transportation services for animals throughout Europe. All three limousine services accept advance reservations. Services like these are in limited supply (not everyone travels by limo, you understand), so it is wise to phone ahead.

WELCOME TO THE RAT RACE
(OFFICE SUPPLIES AND DESK ACCESSORIES)
PAGES 84 TO 85

LAMP, NOTEBOOK, AND LETTER OPENER—Mabel's, 849 Madison Avenue, New York, NY 10021, (212) 734-3263
GARFIELD PHONE—Tyco; for information call 1-800-257-7728
PICTURE FRAMES, SCISSORS, BOOKENDS, PENCILS, PENCIL CUP, TAPE DISPENSER, RULER, NOTE PAPER, AND STAPLER—Cats, Cats & More Cats, P.O. Box 270, Monroe, NY 10950

CATATONIC CATASTROPHE

CATNIP—

THE DRUG PROBLEM

Many cats find the attraction and availability of this mind-altering drug too exciting a combination to handle. They indulge in wanton use, lose perspective and are motivated by powerful urges beyond their control.

By Javanese Junkie

Katmandu* glanced furtively over her shoulder. No one was watching, no one would see. She stalked into the backyard and nestled into her favorite spot, hidden from view. Now she was alone and could finally indulge in her hidden passion. Slowly, she began to nibble upon a nearby plant. The familiar good feeling would soon overtake her, and she chewed faster. Suddenly she rubbed her face against the ground, and her body, as if possessed, started to roll about in the grass. A low moan gave way to more passionate meowing. She no longer cared if anyone could hear or see her in this frantic state. After several minutes, her body relaxed and she lay calm upon the grass. A short rest, and she would begin the whole cycle again....

Snowball* awoke and stretched her front paws. She rolled off her silk brocade cushion and padded into the kitchen. What to eat? Should she try some liver pâté, or was she in the mood for tuna tartare? Suddenly, she remembered the dish of bonbons, the delicious kitty treats. She began with one, but before long, she had another and then another. Soon she gobbled up the entire dish of them with mad abandon. She was out of control, and began to chase phantom butterflies around the room. She leaped and pirouetted across the kitchen counter, barely missing the hot stove, and after several minutes lay crumpled in a tired heap on a kitchen chair. She looked up a few moments later when the maid entered the room. The woman replaced the empty dish with a fresh one filled with bonbons. A brief nap, and she would begin the whole cycle again....

These two cats, while very different in many ways, share a terrible secret: They are both addicted to catnip. They appear to lead normal and happy lives, but their days are not complete without frequent indulgence in powerful, mood-altering drugs. And they are not alone.

Scientific studies have shown that one out of every two cats is born with an addictive personality—the ability to get high on catnip. The trait is hereditary and has nothing to do with conditioning. Young cats under three months old exhibit no response when exposed to these drugs. Older cats, however, are evenly divided into two groups: those who avoid or ignore catnip, and those who are driven to frenzy and eventual stupor through its use.

The catnip plant, also known as catmint, grows as a weed throughout North America and Europe. The plant contains an oil called nepetalactone, which produces an effect similar to that of marijuana or LSD. The user experiences a euphoric feeling and behaves in an uninhibited manner. This may be accompanied by visual and auditory hallucinations; the cat may respond to stimuli which are not really present. Chasing after phantom mice is not unusual, nor are conversations with others when no one else is around. Fortunately, the drug trip lasts for only five to fifteen minutes, and no permanent negative effects have been seen in cats who are "social nippers."

Catnip is available in several forms. It can grow wild or be cultivated in flower pots. Dried leaves are sold, and the essential oils can be obtained in liquid and even aerosol forms. The active ingredients are frequently added to gourmet foods, treats, and even toys. Cats can chew or sniff the "weed," eat the foods and treats, inhale the aroma from toys, and, in extreme cases, get high from sniffing the fumes from aerosol cans. With such easy access to this powerful stimulant, a prudent cat must regulate her exposure to the intoxicant.

Many cats, however, find the attraction and availability of this mind-altering drug too exciting a combination to handle. They indulge in wanton use, lose perspective, and are motivated by powerful urges beyond their control. They ingest the drug in all its potent forms, and spend a good portion of their days high on drug trips. Junkies wake from a drug-induced stupor only to take another dose of catnip. Cats lose their sense of reason and have no regard for meaningful work or activities, preferring another dose of catnip mice to hunting for the real thing.

Some fortunate cats have recognized this downward spiral toward ruin and have sought therapy. Unfortunately, drug treatment centers have not yet been formed to fight these dreadful addictions. There is no 1 (800) CAT-NIPP hotline to provide guidance. The brave catnip junkie must be her own savior in the long battle to combat addiction. But it *can* be done, and many cats have won the fight to live long, drug-free lives. As in all other forms of addiction, the recovering addict is "clean" of the drug but can never be "cured." The cat must remain forever vigilant against the urge to revert to catnip use in a moment of need or weakness. Indeed, social nipping can again become the first step toward addiction and, without care, the whole cycle would begin again....

***The names of the catnip addicts in this article have been changed.**

The Many Forms of Catnip: A Social Nipper's Guide

The natural catnip plant, grown wild, or cultivated in a garden or flower pot (as shown here).

The dried leaves; available commercially in most pet stores.

The toys, stuffed or scented with catnip; available in most pet stores.

Essential catnip oils, packaged in pump or aerosol sprays, to be applied to recipes, playthings, and possessions; available in most pet stores.

The Cat's Out of the Bag—

HE'S PUSSYFOOTING AROUND

By Tiffany Traveler

They appear to be the picture of contented feline family life. The tomcat strong and handsome, his mate fluffy and beautiful, with a litter of playful kittens to complete the idyllic image of a loving, trusting family. But one day we find the blissful image shattered—the mother cat alone at home, the kittens dispersed. And the tomcat—what has become of the tomcat? How did he exit the warm family group?

Closer examination of the opening scene provides us with a better understanding of what has happened here. We have witnessed something that is a simple fact of feline life—marriages seldom last, especially between unneutered cats. Tomcats habitually depart after mating, rarely remaining to witness the birth of their offspring. Tomcats are free to roam at will, and some will exercise this freedom most completely by choosing to travel—to pussyfoot around in new and unexplored territories. Some tomcats will even avail themselves of the help of people, who will take them along on their trips to far-flung locations. Cats ready to roam will reluctantly climb into cat carriers in exchange for the opportunity to travel to new places.

Upon arrival, our seasoned traveler will revert to the free and dominant behavior he enjoyed before. Once the cat's out of the bag, he will forget the indignities of confinement and will proceed to enjoy the novelty of a trip away from home.

The cat traveler has many transportation options. He may travel by air, sea, bus, or car. A cat contemplating a trip, domestic or foreign, should carefully research his mode of travel. Public conveyances have strict rules about animals, and it would be wise to plan ahead. Several booklets are available that provide information on how to travel safely and comfortably while adhering to the rules and regulations set down by individual carriers. These booklets include: "Traveling with Your Pet," available from the ASPCA, Education Department, 441 East 92nd Street, New York, NY 10028, (212) 867-7700; "Traveling with Pets," Consumer Information, United States Travel Service, U.S. Department of Commerce, Washington, D.C. 20230; and "Traveling with Your Cat," The Pet Information Center, 505 Market Street, Knoxville, TN 37902.

A cat may choose to travel away from his people. He may want to stay at one of the nation's many catteries or boarding kennels. The cat contemplating traveling alone would be wise to select a safe and competent "hotel." Many of these are listed in a guidebook produced by the American Boarding Kennels Association. They can provide travelers with two helpful booklets. In addition to the hotel listing already mentioned, the group also offers a booklet called "How to Select a Boarding Kennel." Both brochures can be obtained by contacting the American Boarding Kennels Association, 311 North Union, Colorado Springs, CO 80909 (303) 635-7082. Another interesting thing to read is a new book from Dodd, Mead & Co., called *All The Comforts of Home—The Story of The First Pet Motel* by Robert X. Leeds. Four-legged travelers would be wise to read it to avoid the pitfalls of poorly run pet motels.

Feline frequent travelers may wish to obtain Pet Passports. These look like the official ones issued to people, but they contain pertinent information about health and diet and are an invaluable aid in informing others of your habits and preferences while you are away. You may order one from Innovative Amenities, 1021 Lincoln Blvd., Suite 217, Santa Monica, CA 90403, (213) 394-6992.

While the travel tips given here have been directed at the straying tomcat, what's good for the goose is good for the gander (as they say in bird talk). Female felines would be wise to follow the same guidelines we offer when preparing to fly the coop (more bird talk). Whatever your gender, trips away can be a refreshing opportunity to relax and regain a sense of purrspective. Separate vacations are one way to breathe new life into a foundering relationship. When you are reunited, you may view each other anew and restore the romance for another try at family life.

Carol Purrnet

Brooke Sphynx

Tomcat Cruise

Nastassja Kitty

Woody Alleycat

Cyndi Clawper

WHAT GIVES ME PANGS OF GUILT?

By Cymric Conscience

Tomcat Cruise: *"Nothing."*

Carol Purrnet: *"Nothing."*

Bill Catsby: *"Nothing."*

Nastassja Kitty: *"Nothing."*

Lily Tomcat: *"Nothing."*

Steve Malayan: *"Nothing."*

Catty La Belle: *"Nothing."*

Cyndi Clawper: *"Nothing."*

David Lee Rat: *"Nothing."*

Javanese Rivers: *"Nothing."*

Elizabeth Tailer: *"Nothing."*

Kitty Brinkley: *"Nothing."*

Clawrenzo Lamas: *"Nothing."*

Loni Abyssinian: *"Nothing."*

Katleen Turner: *"Nothing."*

Kelly Meow Gillis: *"Nothing."*

Bill Meowry: *"Nothing."*

Luciano Pawvarotti: *"Nothing."*

Phoebe Cats: *"Nothing."*

Burmese Reynolds: *"Nothing."*

Dudley Manx: *"Nothing."*

Jamie Lee Catis: *"Nothing."*

Brooke Sphynx: *"Nothing."*

Liza Minnie: *"Nothing."*

David Bombay: *"Nothing."*

Larry Himalayan: *"Nothing."*

Ragdoll Duvall: *"Nothing."*

Rex Cat: *"Nothing."*

Turkish Danza: *"Nothing."*

Woody Alleycat: *"Everything."*

Introducing the Flea Furry Rider. The faded blue of stonewashing with a new, rounded silhouette. Made of bleached cotton denim with the easy comfort of your favorite old jeans. And the fit that made Flea famous.
NEW FLEA FURRY RIDER
® M.R.
Flea
THE BRAND FOR FUR

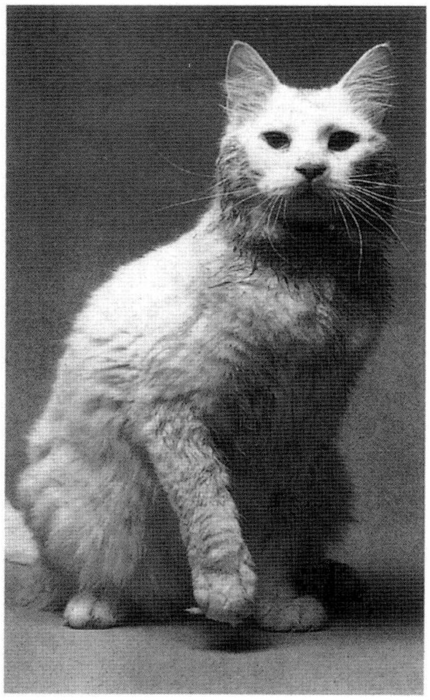

A TALE OF TWO KITTIES

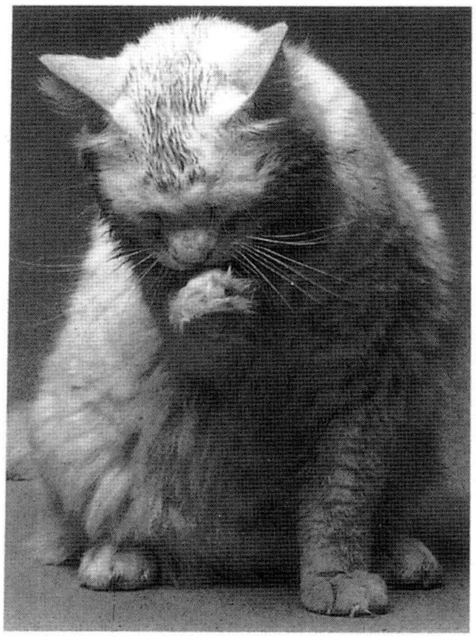

A Cat Can Change Her Spots In 3 Easy Steps!

By Vidal Sinapura

Turkey (an unfortunate name for a Turkish Angora) is a ratty cat. A romp in the garden has left her in a bedraggled state, her fur all spotted with mud. She will be transfurmed into a feline fantasy right before your eyes. You can undergo the same makeover miracle if you follow her simple directions. They entail just 3 easy steps to beauty.

↑ 1. Starting at the top, lick one paw clean and use it to cleanse your face.

← 2. Lick your chest fur with long, even strokes to comb it flat against your body.

→ 3. Paws and claws should be cleaned last, as fur will fly and may leave fluffy deposits on your little cat feet.

Turkey is now a Glamour Puss. She's spotlessly elegant after a little bit of dry cleaning and the recipient of admiring cat calls wherever she goes. You will be, too, lickety split!

PHOTOGRAPHS BY BRUCE PLOTKIN

WHAT'S MEW IN BEAUTY

Don't cry over split claws. The wise CATMO Cat knows how to keep her claws trim with regular pawicures. She uses a specially designed pair of cat-claw scissors to do the task neatly and painlessly. Try this pair, from Hagen, available at pet-supply stores everywhere.

He'll find your odor intoxicating when you apply Cologne of the Wild from Professional Pet Products. The fragrance is sure to bring out the beast in your tomcat! He'll treat you like Cleocatra!

Sensitive skin? Soften and medicate it with Cardinal's luxurious Hot Oil Skin Care System. Cats, more than anyone, deserve pampering, and one treatment will leave your skin moist and dewy, your fur shiny and glossy.

Treat yourself (and a friend) to a bubble bath you'll both remember. A warm and sudsy tumble with Safer Flea Shampoo will leave you both clean, sweet-smelling, and (best of all) pest-free!

Comb your luxurious locks with a specially designed comb from Fleamaster. It has delicate teeth spaced very closely together. The unique design traps and removes fleas with every stroke. So comb your way to beauty, health, and comfort.

ILLUSTRATIONS BY CATHERINE CLAYTON PURNELL

Where to purrchase on last page.

catmo tells all

△ **Cats are the catalyst for love in more ways than one.** Besides providing your people with *cat* love, you can help them find *people* love from other pet lovers! Single Pet Lovers is a way for unattached people who love animals to meet and date people like themselves. For more information, contact Single Pet Lovers, P.O. Box 487, La Guardia, NY 11371.

◁ **Finder of lo pets—** Petfinde is a nonprof national organiz tion that locat missing pet The organizati matches missi and found pe by computer, a circulates a los pet report to animal shelter humane societie and rescue lea ues within a 4 mile radius where the pet w lost. They mai tain a toll-fr 800 number, a answer the phones from 9 5 daily, Easte Standard Tim Register for lif time membersh before it's to late! Phone (80 666-LOST.

△ **You've been called a "real doll," but this time they mean it literally!** Blythe Cats creates handmade, life-sized cats of imitation fur stuffed with Polyfil—and they look just like you! It will never replace the real thing, but two cats are better than one (and *you* can eat *both* dinners!). For more information, call (206) 789-6772, or write to Blythe Designs, P.O. Box 17506, Seattle, WA 98107.

Plush cats ▽ **raise funds for The Humane Society of the United States.** No, we are not refurring to a jaded group of aristocats. We're talking about a collection of stuffed cat toys from Determined Productions, 24 East 22nd Street, New York, NY 10010, (212) 254-6600. A portion of the selling price is given to the HSUS to support its many valuable programs. For more information contact The Humane Society of the United States, 2100 L Street, NW, Washington, DC 20037.

Cat courtship and feline family life ▷ are charmingly pawtrayed in fiberglass copies of antique sculptures at Site, a gift shop that sells display props to cats and their people for home decoration or as unique gifts. Have you ever wanted to purrchase a wonderful prop you saw in a store window or used for display inside the store? Now you can—at Site! Visit Site at 35 North Main Street, New Hope, PA 18938.

Look beneath the surface. The Catter's you loved as a kitten is all grown up. And so are you. The comforting familiar pussy pants are now pared down.

French cut bikinis, hipsters, and strings. They reveal the new you. And put you in the catbird seat. The purrfect addition to the classic Catter's line.

Catter's

A Kitty Event

catmo tells all

Kitty Treats can ▷ now be given to your people when they behave. There's nothing like positive reinforcement in a people-obedience program, and nothing works better than *candy.* People prefer it to catnip! Try the *Big Cat* bar from Rowntree De Met's, Inc., 230 West Monroe Street, Suite 2738, Chicago, IL 60606, (312) 443-0893.

△ **Don't forget to write...** Your social obligations are now made easier when you use a purrsonalized paw-print stamp to sign your correspondence. You can say good-bye to inky paws. The stamp even includes your name, so people can identify your paw-written notes! Order yours from Print Pads, P.O. Box 343, East Ely, NV 89315, (702) 289-6312.

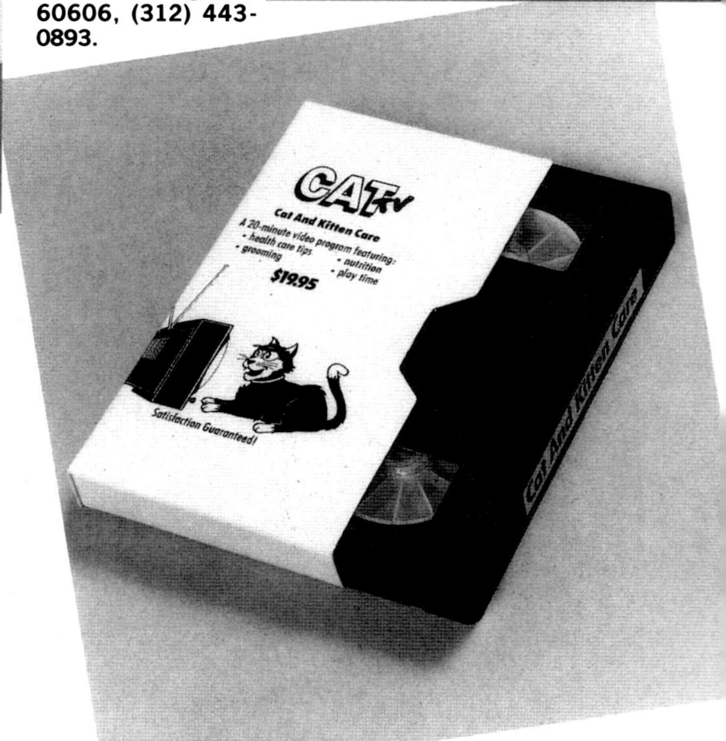

Cat TV We now ▷ have our own 20-minute video program that gives tips on health care, nutrition, grooming, and playtime. It doesn't feature Cyndi Clawper, but it will still hold your interest. Place your order with AV Designs, P.O. Box 1756, Redondo Beach, CA (213) 379-5818.

◁ **The ultimate catalog of cat books—** Books on our favorite subject—cats—are listed in this complete catalog. You never realized so many cat books had been published (though somehow you suspected it all along). To simplify things, they can be purrchased through a single resource. Write to The Cat Book Center, Box 112 Wykagyl Station, New Rochelle, NY 10804. Send $2.00 for a catalog.

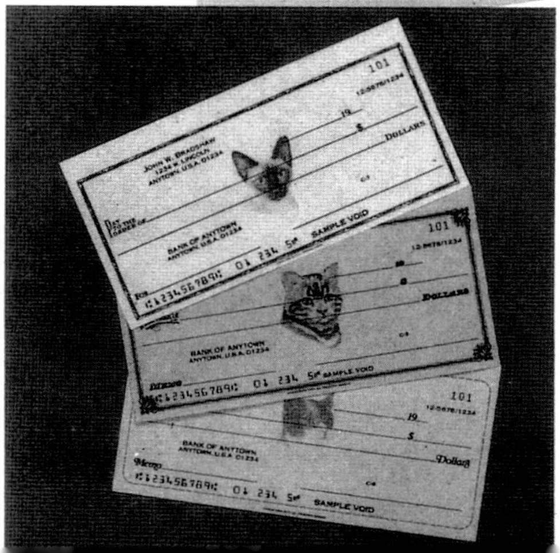

◁ **Check it out!** Purrsonalized bank checks are available in 24 different breeds from the Kansas Bank Note Company. Or send them your own original art or photograph for a design that's yours alone! Contact the Kansas Bank Note Company, P.O. Box 360, Fredonia, KS 66736, (316) 378-3026. Write on!

You are cordially invited to meet (and eat) the adorable, amusing (and very tasty) Mousey Family

AUNT MOUSEY BAKING HER FAMOUS GINGERBREAD MICE

GRANDFATHER OLD MOUSEY

COUNTRY COUSIN MOUSEY

GRANDMA OLD MOUSEY

MOMMA AND POPPA MOUSEY

SISTER MOUSEY, SWEET AS CANDY

BROTHER FARM MOUSEY

A NEW COLLECTION OF DELICATE, PAW-PAINTED PAWCELAIN FIGURINES

There's Grandfather Old Mousey, the patriarch of this great family... Grandma Old Mousey, his lovely wife and the mother of countless children.... They're all here, generations of them, in the Mousey Family. Twenty-five members in all, and still counting....Each lifelike figure is pawtrayed in actual size, no bigger than 3 inches tall. Carefully crafted in imported bisque pawcelain and tenderly painted by paw, the figures capture every detail of character and clothing. Our artists are true mouse-lovers and have handled enough real mice to know and appreciate those small details which might be overlooked by less critical (and knowledgeable) *human* artists.

The Mousey Family is the perfect adornment for your home. Your family will derive many hours of pleasure from examining and handling the members of The Mousey Family. Grow familiar with their faces, appreciate their tiny (and tasty) forms. Best of all, the figures are life-size, so they can be used as decoys to attract real mice into your home when you are training your kittens to hunt. Imagine the fun for your entire family.

The collection is beautifully contained in a wooden "mouse house," which will hold all 25 figurines. And in the tradition of fine families everywhere, the Mousey Family will have a fully illustrated copy of its family tree, complete with a map to help you locate this magical mouse-filled place.

To start collecting your Mousey Family, all you need to do is complete and mail the application by June 30, 1987.

The Mousey Family

Please mail by June 30, 1987

The Furranklin Mint
Furranklin Center, Pennsylvania
XOXOX

Please enter my subscription for "The Mousey Family," consisting of 25 paw-painted figurines.

I need send no payment now. I will receive my collection at the rate of one figurine each month, and I will be billed one dead bird or mouse for each. My collection will include, at no charge, the display "mouse house."

Paw Print ______________________

Name ______________________

Address ______________________

City, State, Zip ______________________

catmo tells all cats

◁ **Snow is a real glamour puss.** Her photograph was taken by Francesco Scavullo. Her makeup is done daily by Akira Mitani, the famous makeup artist (they even live together). What a fortunate feline! People can get the same treatment from Akira by calling his agency—Zoli Illusions, (212) 308-4022. (But he won't do other cats—he's faithful to his favorite feline!)

PHOTOGRAPH BY FRANCESCO SCAVULLO

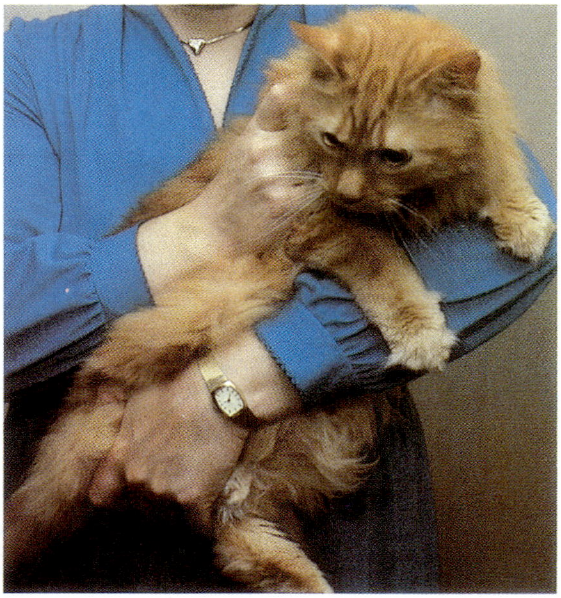

△ **Pumpkin wins the search for The Magical Musical Meow,** and $25,000, from Ralston Purina. The "Meow Off" was held October 30, 1986, at Lincoln Center's Alice Tully Hall. Pumpkin will appear in a Meow Mix cat-food advertisement as part of the grand prize.

TOMCAT OF THE MONTH

▽ **Merlin is a magical tomcat.** He won't reveal his age, but he's in the prime of life. He is co-founder of The Cat Empire, a company that produces postcards that feature him dressed for many different roles. "Magicat" the magician (shown here) and "Peiping Tom," the Chinese emperor, are just two. His partner, Michael Weigall, has written a book about Merlin, called *The Cat Empire,* to be published by England's Corgi Books in the fall of 1987. Pretty pussies can write to him care of G.P. Putnam's Sons, 200 Madison Avenue, New York, NY 10016.

COUPLE OF THE MONTH

REPRINTED WITH SPECIAL PERMISSION OF KING FEATURES SYNDICATE, INC.

◁ **Krazy Kat and Ignatz** are the proverbial "brick-crossed" lovers. Maybe one day Krazy Kat will get her beloved mouse. We can only hope for the best.... You can read about these famous almost-lovers in a book from Harry N. Abrams, called *Krazy Kat: The Comic Art of George Herriman.*

CAREER CORNER

Mabel was a simple shop girl who went ▷ on to fame and fortune. She was the inspiration behind the popular Madison Avenue boutique that bears her name. Many of the items sold in the store carry her image (and those items seem to sell best!). Visit the store at 849 Madison Avenue, N.Y., NY 10021.

CATNIP DIP MADE EASY CATBELL'S SOUP/DIPS

Catbell's makes it easy for you to create great dips in moments.

The recipe is on the label. See just how easy it is.

CATBELL SOUP/DIP RECIPE

Catnip Great hot or cold.

For a hot dip, heat a can of Catbell's Catnip Soup and pour over fish treats.

For a cold dip, mix one can of Catbell's Catnip Soup with sour cream. Serve with a garnish of dried catnip, and a platter of dried sardines for dipping.

Your next party will have new purrpose when you whisk up these dips.

CATBELL'S
SOUP MAKES CAT FOOD.

MANUFACTURER'S COUPON	NO EXPIRATION DATE

13¢ OFF CATBELL'S
NEW CATNIP SOUP

13¢ OFF 123456 00051

The Paws That Refreshes

Isn't it lovely to curl up in a beautiful bed? Selecting a bed is a very purrsonal choice that reflects your taste and purrsonality. So, paws and think carefully before choosing the bed that will tell him about you. And remember, the CATMO Cat would be wise to consider his *taste as well.... You'll often snuggle up in that bed* together! *Sweet dreams!*

1. A red plush heart is the purrfect valentine of love for your tomcat.

2. Wildcats will delight in a seductive cave of faux fur.

3. Outdoorsy cats will snuggle on a rustic tartan quilt on cold winter nights.

PHOTOGRAPHS BY BRUCE PLOTKIN

4. Romantic rosebuds and ribbon form a nostalgic wallpaper stripe in this bed shaped like a Russian hat.

5. Curl up in a delicate floral nest edged in luxurious lace.

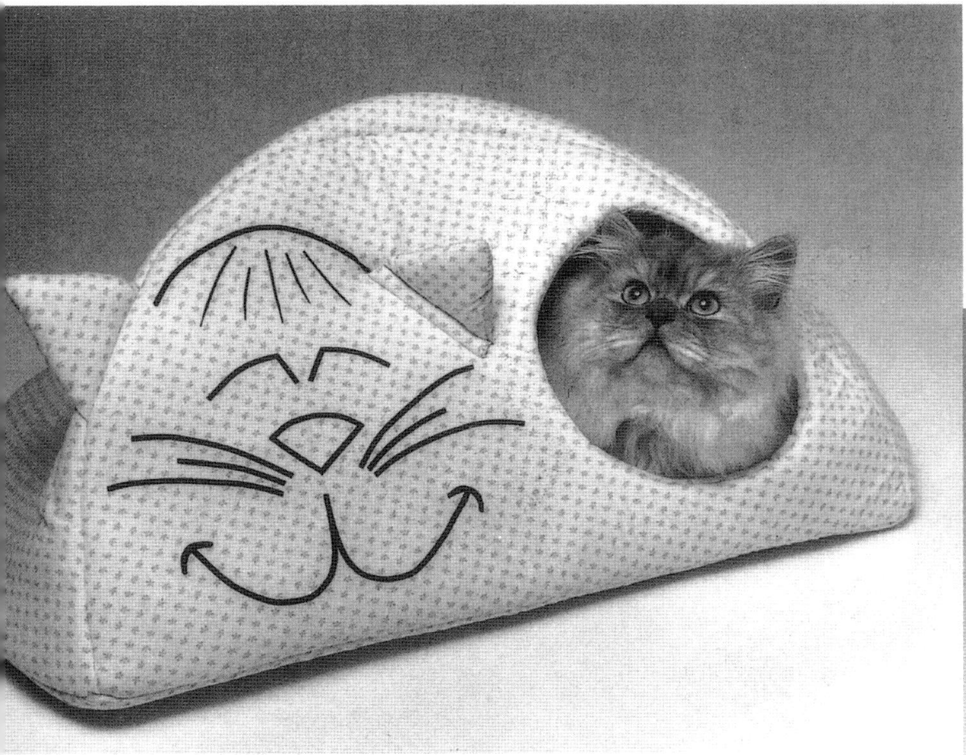

6. A happy cat forms your calico hideaway.

7. A tisket, a tasket, it's chintz inside a basket!

Where to purrchase on last page.

CAT HOUSES: SLEEP WITH THE BEST

1. The Catbird Seat gives all animals living together a safe place to go. A real kitty condo, it comfortably houses a bird (top), cat (center), and mouse (bottom). The dog must resort to a home of his own.

The cagey CATMO Cat has an eye for real estate. She knows value and will always choose to bed down with the best. Our CATMO Cat won't settle; she'll select her home with care to reflect her taste and protect her investment. CATMOPOLITAN presents a vast selection of designer homes—best bets for pets!

3. Catnastics is a jungle gym for cats.

2. A faux-malachite home features post-modern design. A silk cushion provides creature comfort. . . .

4. A clean, modern table conceals your home. A way to stay at the center of activity, but slip away when you choose.

5. The Spanish colonial design provides you with an elegant place to receive your guests.

6. An Egyptian temple suggests a home worthy of a cat god. Or goddess—*you*. . . .

7. A Persian temple reflects your Oriental origins.

8. The English cottage is a simple design, purrfect for weekends in the country with friends.

Where to purrchase on last page.

↑9. A cat's home is her castle. . . . Give yourself the royal treatment!

10. The purrfect place for a post-modern puss. . . . "Even the wildest animals love comfort": Thoreau. ↑

↓11. Religious cats will devote themselves to this cozy chapel.

12. Country cats are comfortable in their barn . . . the hayloft is filled with field mice! ↑

↑13. A kitty castle lets you reign over your yard in style.

14. With the Catnap Hotel, you can slip away for a brief vacation...in the comfort of your own home! ↑

↓15. The Cat-er-Ciser resembles a two-story tract house. Build yours close to a handsome neighbor's!

THE TOMCAT—WHAT CAN SHE SEE IN HIM?

BY LONI ABYSSINIAN

HIS ANIMAL MAGNETISM MAKES PUSSYCATS SWOON

But we have that sinking feline that no one can tame this wildcat….

That Catmopolitan Male

BURMESE REYNOLDS

Good Mousekeeping

Pawcelain bowls with coordinating place mats let you set a pretty floor for guests...or for yourself. Good looks combine with easy care for the CATMO Cat on the go—the bowls are dishwasher safe, the mats lick clean. Pamper yourself with one of these beautiful sets of dinnerware—it will even make canned food look appetizing!

1. The mat is set with faux cutlery. The bowl is screened with "Have a Mice Meal."

2. The Haute Feline signature dinnerware set comes in elegant gray-and-silver—the understated look for well-bred aristocats.

PHOTOGRAPHS BY BRUCE PLOTKIN

3. ● Kliban cats adorn the whimsical feeder—an informal look for quick snacks. Purrfect for a weekend home.

4. ● "Good Kitty" dishes have a French-country look with blue-on-white checks and stripes.

5. ● Primary brights in a naïve and playful cat design—the purrfect look for kittens.

Where to purrchase on last page.

Playing Cat and Mouse

1.

2.

Cat toys bring out the kitten in every cat! Whether they are enhanced with a catnip fragrance or take on the playful shapes of familiar prey like mice, food, or slippers, toys entice us to catch as cats can. Drop out of the rat race for a few minutes to bat around a catnip mouse... and you'll be grinning like a Cheshire cat before long. So buy a toy like one of these, or be the cat's meow and buy the whole kitten caboodle!

Where to purrchase on last page.

PHOTOGRAPHS BY BRUCE PLOTKIN

3.

4.

1. A real rats-to-riches story—catnip mice in Ultrasuede®!
2. Cosmic catnip mice in colorful calico prints.
3. High-tech catnip mice in dots and stripes.
4. Space Mouse and Dress-Up Mouse are only two cartoon mice from a series of seven.

5. Have a heart. Send this catnip valentine to your favorite kitty. (It's better than a chocolate-filled one!)

5.

6.

6. A mouse hides in a wedge of cheese, while the cat peeks out of a paper bag, illustrating the old saying, "While the cat's away, the mice will play."

7. Momma said, "Don't play with your food." Bad kittens can misbehave with these catnip food toys.

7.

8.

8. Don't tear up your people's slippers—yours are tastier, and scented with catnip.

Scratch 'n' Sniff

Scratching Posts can come out of the closet! These new designs are attractive additions to any decor and add a humorous touch of whimsy to any home. Avoid a catastrophe—purrchase a scratching post before things get too claw-strophobic and you find yourself whiskered away to the veterinarian!

Catbirds feel more at home in a tree. And so will you when you choose this rustic scratching post from American Cat Emporium, P.O. Box 745, Elburn, IL 60119, 1(800) 75AMCAT

Country cats tell tall cat tales in a Pennsylvania Dutch barn. A traditional hex sign keeps the bad spirits of people away from your private "tearitory." Best Friend Products, 940 New Market Street, Philadelphia, PA 19123, (215) 627-5555.

Having a swinging time, wish you were here to join in the fun on our cat gyms. Two designs of this cat fur-niture can be purrchased from Booda Products, 439 South Detroit Street, Los Angeles, CA 90036, (213) 939-9149.

A kitty car can train you to sharpen your claws quickly and easily. Three railroad cars let you choo-choose a good place to exercise your scratching desires. The train is only one of many scratching post designs. Other fast-track designs include the airplane, riverboat, and horse, also shown here. With all these choices, don't get carried away! JG Enterprises, 713 Taylor Street, Elkhart, IN 46516, (219) 522-2474.

THE CAT'S PAJAMAS: FELINE FANTASIES SLIP OUT AT NIGHT

The Catmo Cat knows how to purrsuade her mate to purrform.... She's on the prowl and looking hotter than ever in feline lingerie too pretty to stay in the bedroom....

Lavender and Old Lace is the purrfect combination. A nostalgic bed jacket (left) covers the satin bodice, while the graceful lace skirt billows around fluffy feet. Vanity Fur.

Aqua lace, cool as ice, slips over satin (right). The low-cut surplice wrap bodice reveals ample cat cleavage; the frothy lace skirt leaves little to the imagination. Maidenfur.

Photographs by Bruce Plotkin

Alexis beware...Kitty glitter was never like this! Black and gold metallic lace (left) forms a sleek kimono over a slip of a satin gown. Nolan Millpurr.

Cream lace pours over satin in a romantic evening ensemble (right). Every cat's favorite color (and flavor), cream mixes well with all fur colors, bringing out the best in every one. Lily of Furance.

Sweet dreams are made of this. Clouds of white lace spill from a pearl-buttoned pink satin camisole (left). Kittenish innocence purrsonified. . . .
Cheshire Dior.

Cat on a Red-Hot Tin Roof. Red lace ruffles slide off the shoulder (right). A satin gown fit for a wildcat...like you.
Calvin Claw.

Welcome to the Rat Race:

THE BUSINESS ANIMAL IN THE CORPURRATE BATTLEFIELD

Hiss Claiborne
Fashion Designer

Being a designer has its moments. I purrticularly enjoy having the oppurrtunity to shape fashion trends. Who ever expected to see a magazine like CATMOPOLITAN or feline fashion (except for collars) several seasons ago?! The industry is growing by leaps and bounds, and I am thrilled to be one of the founding felines of contemporary cat clothing. My proudest moment came when I completed work with Simplicity Patterns on their first home-sewing pattern for cat clothing. I can't wait for my cat couture to appear in *Harpurr's Bazaar!*

Kitty Brinkley
Model

I enjoy being a model, but it is not always as glamorous as it appears to be. I have to get up early on the day of a shoot, and I am immediately subjected to a *bath.* No, not a soothing, luxurious tongue bath that I leisurely purrform myself, but a bath in a tub full of water, with *shampoo!* Oh, the price we pay for beauty! Sometimes the day is long and boring, but I love the chance to meet creative cats and to be the first cat to wear the new season's fashions. I've recently signed a contract with a new brand of kitty treats to appear in commercials as their spokescat. I'm hoping for a more fulfilling career. I'd like to purrsue acting roles—this cat can growl, and I'd love to unleash my emotions on film!

Roberta Purrina
Dietician

I'm a professional Fat Cat. I got this way by being the best in the business. I'm a food taster for a major cat-food company. My job is to try the new flavors of cat food and evaluate them for appearance and palatability. My problem is that I like almost every flavor I eat, even the unusual ones like Tuna in Peanut Butter Sauce. (I thought it was Japanese, like sushi. And cold noodles with sesame sauce has always been one of my favorites....) The company loves me because I eat almost everything that is set before me. I guess they can thank me for helping to increase their line to more than 25 flavors!

"Spike" Shorthair
Exterminator

I represent the blue-collar cat. I work in a factory as a mouser to keep the environment pest-free. My job is a very important one—the rat race would be lost without cats like me. Remember the black plague? That's what can happen without mousers. We've recently organized into a union. We call ourselves the "teemsters" because the factories would be teeming with mice without us. We've been working for below minimum wage—we get to eat all the mice we catch—but we're tired of getting only "furbacks." We'd like to see some "greenbacks" for a change! If conditions don't improve, we'll call a "wildcat strike."

Muffy Vanpurrbilt
Feline Philanthropist

I am a fund-raiser for cat causes. I do good work for organizations like the ASPCA and animal shelters. I was born into a well-to-do family, and my mother taught me to share my good fortune with others less fortunate than myself. My pet causes are the hungry and the homeless. I am an advocat for any organization that will provide these stray cats with nourishment and shelter. I may seem demure, but I can fight like a tiger for the rights of my fellow cats.

Benita Catsey
Pet Therapist

I have always been fascinated by the bond between people and their pets, a relationship which is mutually beneficial. The animals receive food, shelter, and daily care in exchange for the attention and affection they offer. Certain mutual medical benefits can also be derived—the people can provide regular veterinary attention for their animals while enjoying lower blood pressure from interacting with their pets. I am a volunteer in a program that provides animal companionship to elderly people in a retirement home. I love to visit my "grandparents" every week because each visit gives us all so much pleasure.

Mabel Mixedbreed
Retailer

I am the proprietor of a luxurious boutique. The store features merchandise with an animal motif for people. They are suckers for a pretty face like mine! I'm told that any item in the store sells better if it has my image on it. That's why you'll find everything, from rugs to mugs, with my face on it. It's lucky that all this adulation hasn't gone to my head! If it had, I wouldn't have the time or attention to devote to all my daily responsibilities. Running a store is exciting, but it involves long hours of hard work. Any copycat can emulate my ideas, but it takes almost nine lives of dedication to leap to the top.

Elizabeth Tailer
Show Business

There's no business like show business.... But behind the kitty glitter lurks a lot of time spent clawing your way up.... Cat shows are a difficult field to break into. A cat must possess beauty, purrsonality, and patience, because the road to the "Best of the Best" is long and filled with broken claws and dreams. The other contestants can be catty, and fur often flies. But there is no feeling like the moment when your name is announced and, tail held high, your paw is raised in victory. It makes the whole rat race seem worthwhile.

The business animal remains top cat by keeping her office letter-purrfect. A feline executive likes her desk to reflect her purrsonality, like the desk shown here. Accessories have been selected with an eye for design and function. This kitty corner says you can't play cat and mouse with *this* feline executive! Sources for the office supplies and desk accessories shown here are given on the last page.

A CAT'S NINE LIVES

COLORFUL COLLARS TO CATCH HIS EYE!

Watch the birdie
An exotic collar sets the mood for the hunt. Our fine-feathered friends were never more helpful. By Nolan Millpurr.

Don't pussyfoot around....The CATMO Cat has only nine lives to live to the fullest! Take the cat by the tail and purrsue *your* elusive tomcat, wearing a colorful collar like one of these to catch his eye. Happy hunting!

The catcalls will be hard to resist
When you wear this black collar that spells out *Kitty Cat* in brightest letters. Look who's in the catbird seat now! By Hiss Claiborne.

These collar designs can be sewn at home. Pattern available from Simplicity Patterns.

PHOTOGRAPHS BY BRUCE PLOTKIN

Zigzag with zip
This collar will bring out the wildcat in your tomcat. By Albert and Purrl Nippaw.

They'll all cheer for the pompom cat
Pompoms in vivid colors punctuate a black collar. The cat's meow—pow! By Anne Klaw II.

Purrple passion
A simple but sophisticated design that will turn a few heads. He'll be certain to purrsue you.... By Evan Pawcone.

Kitty glitter
A thick ruff of metallic fringe will make the wildest cat purr with delight (we're not lion!). By Abyssinian Vittadini.

Be a star
Silvery stars shine brightly, but none as bright as you. Show your star quality in this elegant collar by Blasspurr.

A true aristocat
Demonstrate good breeding. Golden lockets discreetly conceal the faces of all your beaux. A thoughtful design by Gloria Vanpurrbilt.

You'll be there with bells on
And so will he! (Ring my chimes.) By Purry Ellis.

Hollywood
HOUSECATS

ILLUSTRATION BY MIMI VANG OLSEN

Supermodel Jade Javanese has moved to Los Angeles to lick her wounds after an unhappy affair with a British shorthair—and Jack Persian, the housecat of a famous talk-show host, is going to ***catch her fancy....***

By Jackie Collars

Jack Persian stalked through the lobby of the Beverly Hills Hotel, all cats' eyes upon him. He had grace, balance, a quiet kind of power, razor-sharp claws, and fur. It all showed.

He was well built with feline good looks. Thick black fur worn just a tad uncombed, mysterious green eyes, a thick ruff of hair spilling over his collar, and a large compact body. He was nine years old, and the world was his.

Jack Persian was the housecat of the most famous talk-show host in America.

"Hello, Jack," purred a slinky cat in a glittering rhinestone collar.

He flashed his killer smile; he had sharp white teeth. He returned her gaze, allowing his penetrating green eyes to purrceive every curve of her body. Standard cat call: "How are you doing, Kitty?"

She began to tell him, but without breaking his graceful gait he just kept stalking toward the Polo Lounge.

Several more cats called out to him along the way. A tourist's cat raised a paw and stared, and a very thin cat in a red collar waved her tail. Jack continued to prowl toward his destination. He leaped into the cozy leather booth facing the door of the Polo Lounge. Table number one—his catbird seat.

A cat was already curled up there. A cat with a slightly confused look, as though suddenly awakened from a deep sleep, clad in fluffy white fur, with cocoa-tipped features. Jack curled up beside him. "Hiya, Himalayan," he meowed.

"Hiya, Jack," Himalayan Solomon meowed back. There was something about the incessant darting of his eyes around the room that gave him a crazed look. Always searching, flashing his eyes, twitching his whiskers. In repose, he was quite good-looking—the soft features relaxed when he was asleep, the even breathing moved his whiskers rhythmically. When awake, however, the constant searching betrayed his high-strung nature. "Where were you last night?" he purred, nervously licking a paw.

"I strolled into a screening at the Katzes'," Jack replied. "It was *Pussy's Honor*. Rex Cat, the reviewer, was there, and he loved it. I just think he's hot for Katleen Turner...."

"I could have told you that," Himalayan purred smugly, "but why spoil your fun? You get off on your nocturnal travels. What would you do without your night stalking? You'd probably just sit alone in your yard and yowl at the moon!"

"You're being pretty catty," Jack meowed. "No film is good these days unless it comes from *your* studio. If it stars Siamese Anderson or another leading lady cat from Oriental Studios, you pronounce it *'Purrfect!'*"

Himalayan licked his other paw and flashed his blue eyes at Jack. "You're right. Our films *are* purrfect! Now let's order our drinks. I'm positively parched!"

"So am I." Jack summoned the waiter and meowed, "Two dishes of cream, no ice."

Saturday morning breakfast at the Polo Lounge had once been the regular stalking ground of Jack and Himalayan and Maine Coon Cat Cable, the television star, who had not yet arrived. Now they were all busy purrsuing their own careers, and it was a rare occasion when they could find time for a drink together.

Himalayan was the housecat of the head of Oriental Studios. He had always enjoyed the power, and now that he had the run of the studio in addition to the Bel Air estate, he was truly in his element. "Top Cat" was a nickname he found easy to answer to....

Scratching at the top of the table with ragged claws, Himalayan glanced catty-cornered at Jack and broke into a Cheshire cat grin. "How's Clarissa?" he purred.

Jack's fur bristled slightly. "She didn't attend the screening. She can be pretty catty. Unless she's in the movie or was offered the part and turned it down, she has no purrpose for it. I've tried to tame her, but you know what they say—a cat can't change her spots."

"Pussycats!" Himalayan spat.

"The whole kitten caboodle...." Jack agreed. "She was pleased with her decision last night. She pounced on me when I got home, and looked like the cat that ate the canary after she'd heard about the film. The part wasn't for her. She's no sex kitten."

Clarissa British Blue was one fierce feline. A serious actress, she had turned out for every catsting call—from cat-food commercials to *Cat on a Hot Tin Roof*. She had endured the indignities of show business—the pawing, the catsting couch—and held her tongue. Always the aristocat, she was cagey while she purred and clawed her way to the top. And now she was there. She had the tiger by the tail; the industry was hers. The darling of the foreign press, she was due to be interviewed by the posh London magazine *Catler*, which planned a feature story for the upcoming issue. She would show them back home. Once she had been an unwanted stray in London, but today she was the cat's meow. A real rats-to-riches story. And Jack Persian, the most desirable housecat in Hollywood, was hers....

Jack pawed his beard. He hardly noticed that his ruffled appearance made him more attractive to the female felines. Ah, those felines...the story of his life. Who would have guessed that he, Jack, the runt of the litter, would grow into the powerful tomcat he was today? He was a passionate Persian, and had long ago lost count of his conquests. The penetrating stare of his green eyes was hypnotic. Pussycats were powerless in his presence. He was often on the prowl for a stray piece of tail, but he always returned home to Clarissa. She was good for him, a chance for him to regain purrspective, to paws and reflect upon his life. But even this exercise in good mousekeeping was beginning to wear thin, and he was growing bored. Curiosity was killing this cat, and it was time for him to return to the streets. This tomcat was ready to stalk....

"Where's Maine?" Jack meowed finally. "Isn't he coming?"

"He does every day," Himalayan purred slyly. "We don't call him 'Kitten-Killer' for nothing."

"You're right." Jack smiled.

Maine Coon Cat Cable was a star with a capital S. When he entered a room, cats took notice, especially the ones that counted. Maine was the star of a popular television series, "Miami Mice." His looks were legendary—the rough-and-tumble air of adventure combined with the classic good looks of his breeding to create an aura that was unique and powerful. A strong hero who was also loving and sensitive. The kittens ate it up. His influence extended beyond the television screen. He was on every list of Top Ten Tomcats, and his informal manner of dress, not unlike the stripes of a raccoon, was copied by cats everywhere. One swish of his fluffy striped tail left the pussies swooning....

Maine finally made his entrance. His eyes were golden. His fur long and glossy. His color a tawny blond striped with brown. His body powerful. One foot tall, nineteen inches long. "Every inch a winner," he'd purr on his frequent late-night talk-show appearances.

He was eight years old. Fit. Fast. And right up there, careerwise, with Morris and Garfield. Yes, Maine Coon Cat Cable was on top with his tail held high....

"I'm hungry enough to eat a canary. What's for breakfast?" Maine growled.

"Mice," replied Jack, eyeing a furry morsel.

Himalayan had been through several mates—he'd almost lost count. Purrple was his current companion. Himalayan had kittens everywhere; Maine was still crazy about his first mate, Pussy Willow, and his new one, Malayan-Shanna, had not yet dimmed the wild look in his eyes or the twinge in his heart. Jack had Clarissa, although he already knew he was beginning to stray.

"Hey, cats," Maine meowed, "how about unleashing our animal magnetism? Let's whisker down to Vegas to have some fun. Roam the town. Chase a little tail. Chew a little grass. Act like wildcats again. Just the three of us. What do you say?" He paused, tail trembling in anticipation.

"Without our mates?" Himalayan purred anxiously.

"You bet your catnip," Maine meowed. "Fur may fly, but we're in this together. A night on the town. Just us, kitten around!"

Himalayan grinned. "I'm all for it. How about you, Jack?"

Jack had promised Clarissa a quiet evening at home. A cat walk in the yard. Mouse and garden. A cat nap, and then the whole kitten caboodle. A purrfect night together. Still, the offer was tempting....

"Yes. Count me in," Jack agreed, eager thoughts on the fun-filled evening ahead, pussy galore....

Jade Javanese was wild about Cat Stevens. She played his tape of greatest hits, *Footsteps in the Dark*, until it was muffled from wear. She knew the songs by heart and meowed along happily, her meows often overpowering the mild purrs coming from the tape.

Jade Javanese was four years old. She had shaggy cream hair with copper markings, penetrating blue eyes, a small pink mouth, and a chiseled, angular face that transformed her from simply beautiful into a striking and unforgettable feline.

She was ten inches tall and weighed nine pounds, with long slender legs, a slim elegant body, a thin, tapered tail, and a graceful, swanlike neck.

Aloof with strangers, she was loyal to her friends, charming and witty, sometimes displaying a wild streak. She was also highly intelligent, independent, and one of the highest-paid models in the world.

The doorbell rang and Jade Javanese leaped off the sofa and darted under the coffee table. She watched curiously as the moving man carried the last of the cartons into the apartment. She was once again grateful for her looks and luck, for the combination had brought her fame and fortune, along with a doting person to handle all life's mundane details. She could enjoy life without having to attend to any of the annoying chores necessary to maintain her carefree existence. Her home was beautiful and well furnished, and her meals were plentiful and varied. What more could she want? And all in exchange for a few hours spent luxuriating before the camera. Not a bad arrangement.

It hadn't always been this easy, but she tried to forget the bad times. She blocked out the long years of hardship, when she'd had to endure the rigors of show business—the cat-show circuit. Confined to a cage, with strange inquiring fingers poking at her. Noisy, rude people keeping her awake while they asked countless questions about her background and breeding. Then the time she spent confined in a carrier, traveling to and from the countless cat shows. It was enough to make one lose purrspective and purrpose....

And, as if this wasn't bad enough, she was then "discovered" and taken out on innumerable catsting calls. The pain of rejection had diminished after the first few months—they had used her body, but they would never control her mind. Long months making the rounds of talent and ad agencies. All in purrsuit of the lucky break—the right match of cat and catalog, pussy and product.

Then one day, when she had finally abandoned all hope of a successful modeling career, it happened. She wasn't even especially trying to catch anyone's attention, but her aloof attitude must have purrsuaded them to select her from the dozens of hopeful cats assembled. She was going to be the spokescat for a new line of cat food. Her indifferent attitude intrigued them. She was *beyond* finicky—she was selective and discriminating. She seemed to embody a serene and ethereal quality—a mystery that held the account executives spellbound. She was fascinating, riveting. She was to become the face of Magnificent Meals.

Soon her days were spent in great luxury and comfort. A plush carrier replaced the crude plastic box. Meals included all varieties of exotic ingredients. She grew to love poached salmon and crab cocktail and lost her taste for mice. The desire even to chase rodents disappeared completely as new culinary delights appeared, without the attendant burdens of hunting and killing. She wore beautifully designed collars and slept in a hand-crafted bed. And now she had moved across the country to California, to appear in a series of commercials introducing the new foods to the great American cat public.

All these changes were welcome ones. She embraced the opportunity of a fresh beginning in Los Angeles, anxious to start her life again where she was known to no one. She had an opportunity to invent herself—to create a new and exciting purrsona. To put all that had gone before behind her. She had her reasons. She welcomed the chance to shed her old life like so much old fur, and begin anew.

She would forget him. Forget that he had ever existed. Forget that they had once been in love. Forget what he had meant to her, done to her.

Meow Rand. An English shorthair. An English rat. The cat of a famous photographer who had photographed her for many of her earliest assignments. They had met in his studio two years ago when she went to pose for a spread in a well-known catalog. He had short gray hair, large green eyes, and he purred incessantly at her. She couldn't help but notice him, and had trouble concentrating on the camera. In fact, she often wandered off the set, and nearly lost the assignment. It took a lot of strength to ignore his plaintive cries. But she did. And when the shoot was over, she scampered off the seamless in search of her mystery suitor. She found him curled up against a spotlight, basking in its remaining warmth. The attraction was strong, immediate, and mutual. They spent the next glorious months together at every opportunity. It wasn't until she had grown deeply attached to him that he mentioned he already had a mate—a cat who lived with him at the photographer's. Furrona Rand. Making the revelation more bitter, she discovered that they even had a litter of kittens who were barely weaned when she first met him!

He made promises, promises. He would leave Furrona when the kittens were older....

And Jade Javanese, smart sophisticat, hardly an innocent kitten, believed that Mickey Mouse nonsense! For two years she'd believed him—and would have continued to believe him if she hadn't heard that Furrona was expecting another litter. *His* litter. She could have scratched his eyes out!

The end came swiftly—her move to California was a welcome relief.

She glanced around the apartment. All her favorite things were still packed in the boxes piled around the living room. Couldn't her handler work faster? She was ready for a nap and would have to settle for curling up on the new sofa. Where was her bed with its comforting, familiar fragrance? Would that woman never finish unpacking? With a sigh, she curled up on the sofa and shut her eyes.

The scratching at the window awakened her from a deep sleep. Jade rubbed her eyes. She did not believe what she was seeing.

Could that be her great friend, Abyssinia, at the window? She knew that he traveled around, but she had no idea that he, too, had settled in Los Angeles. What a wonderful surprise. Things were beginning to look up!

Abyssinia was the crazy cat of a famous New York photographer who had moved to the West Coast to begin a career photographing Hollywood stars. Abyssinia was a flighty cat, but full of fun. He was totally unpredictable, but that was part of his charm. Jade invited him in, and he slipped into the open living room window from the balcony.

"Jade, darling, what are you doing in L.A., my pet?" Abyssinia purred. "How's Meow?"

"He's history!" Jade spat. Regaining her composure, she asked, "How's your boyfriend?"

Abyssinia had so many boyfriends in so little time, Jade had difficulty in remembering their names. So she began to refer to them nebulously—preferring to be safe rather than sorry.

"He's history!" Abyssinia retorted with a quick shake of his tail.

"Well, that makes two of us." She grinned in agreement. "What have you been doing with yourself?"

"Darling, there are so many parties and so many tomcats! I haven't had a quiet night since I arrived here two months ago! There's going to be a wonderful party tonight. Promise me you'll come along. It's a birthday party for a *cat*. They actually throw parties for us here. Why, it's almost like ancient Egypt! The party is for the cat of a famous actress—the cat's name is Siamese Anderson. Everyone will be there, and I'm dying to introduce you to all my new friends. Please come," Abyssinia mewed.

Jade glanced across the living room. The woman was *still* unpacking boxes, and from the look of things, she would be unpacking boxes for the rest of the night. Jade would never be missed.

"Okay," she hissed mischievously, "let's go." And they slipped out the window, onto the balcony, and into the night.

Nora, a Norwegian forest cat, lived with one of Hollywood's most influential publicity agents. Nora knew them all and most of their secrets. She couldn't believe her luck when Jack Persian arrived with Clarissa British Blue. She would have to arrange for Jack to sit next to Siamese Anderson for a single publicity shot. They had never been photographed together.

Few in Hollywood suspected that Jack and Siamese had anything in common. They weren't friends, and traveled in different circles. But, despite their many differences, they had one thing in common. Their mother.

Jack and Siamese were brother and sister. Born in the same litter. From different fathers. Siamese was not really a Siamese at all. Her father was a Siamese, all right, but her mother was a Persian. The resulting kitten had the fine Oriental features and coloring of her father, but a full coat of hair similar to her mother's. She was more an exotic longhair, but she continued to be called by her original name—Siamese.

Jack, on the other hand, was the offspring of two Persian cats and therefore bore little resemblance to his sister. They had little in common and they never mixed socially. He liked it that way. He had come, reluctantly, to her birthday party at the insistence of Clarissa, who knew the secret of their birth and was curious about his sister. He grumbled under his breath at the imposition, but he had agreed to this evening to keep Clarissa happy. She knew about his plans for an evening out with "the toms" and was being very understanding about his needs. How could he deny her this one simple request?

Jade and Abyssinia arrived at the party fashionably late, and made a dramatic entrance. All cats' eyes were upon the couple as they crept into the room. "Who is that ravishing creature?" someone purred under his breath.

"She's magnificent," another concurred.

Jade felt like blushing. She was accustomed to flattering attention, but it had never been as bold or outspoken as this. Things were different in Hollywood. They let the cat out of the bag and let it all hang out. Why, even the mode of dress was different here—the room was awash with fantastic collar creations and all forms of kitty glitter. Yes, it was different, but Jade could see she was going to like it here.

Sashaying around the room, Jade surveyed the scene. Abyssinia was right. There were *so* many toms.

The room was full of married men, with women not their wives. And cats. So many cats. So many with their eyes upon her. She grew warm from the attention and glanced across the room, looking for the door. It was then that she noticed him. A strong and handsome black Persian with electric green eyes. He had noticed her, too; she felt herself flush even warmer. But unafraid, she held his gaze and returned it defiantly. Soon this glittering town would be hers, and so would he. . . .

© 1986.

WHERE TO PURRCHASE: WHAT'S MEW IN BEAUTY
PAGE 57

CAT CLAW SCISSORS—Rolf C. Hagen Corp., P.O. Box 634, Mansfield, MA 02048
COLOGNE OF THE WILD—Professional Pet Products, 1873 NW 97th Avenue, Miami, FL 33172
CARDINAL'S HOT OIL SKIN CARE SYSTEM—Cardinal Laboratories Inc., 710 Ayon Avenue, Azusa, CA 91702
SAFER'S FLEA SHAMPOO—Safer, Inc., 60 Williams Street, Wellesley, MA 02181
FLEAMASTER FLEA COMB—Breeders Equipment Co., Box 177, Flourtown, PA 19031

WHERE TO PURRCHASE: CAT NAPS
(CAT BEDS)
PAGES 64 TO 65

CATNAPPING SIGN—Mabel's, 849 Madison Avenue, New York, NY 10021, (212) 734-3263
RED PLUSH HEART, FAUX FUR, AND TARTAN-PLAID BED—Segy Products available at Harrods, Knightsbridge, London England, and Selfridges, 400 Oxford Street, London, England
ROSEBUD AND RIBBON "HAT" AND LACE-TRIMMED FLORAL NEST—Designer Pet Products, P.O. Box 1867, Hollywood, FL 33022, (305) 922-7060
HAPPY CAT CALICO BED—Our Best Friends, 79 Albertson Avenue, Albertson, NY 11507, (516) 742-7400
BASKET BED—Spunky's Favorite, 484 West 43rd Street, Suite 8C, New York, NY 10036, (212) 244-5158

WHERE TO PURRCHASE: CAT HOUSES
PAGES 66 TO 69

ALL HOUSES ON PAGES 66 AND 67 ARE BY ANIMAL MANORS. Available from Site, 35 North Main Street, New Hope PA 18938
Pages 68 and 69:
CAT CASTLE—Catelot Pet Products, 633 Post Street, Suite 651, San Francisco, CA 94109
POST-MODERN HOUSE, THE ARCHIPET HOME—Upscale, P.O. Box 390545, Mountain View, CA 94039
CHAPEL, BARN, AND KITTY CASTLE—Johnson Creek Products, 1934 Johnson Creek Road, Barker, NY 14012
THE CATNAP HOTEL—The Chatco Collection, P.O. Box 59, Batesville, IN 47006
THE CAT-ER-CISER—The Wun Corporation, 7181 Woodbine Avenue, Suite 114, Markham, Ontario, Canada L3R 1A3

WHERE TO PURRCHASE: GOOD MOUSEKEEPING
(CAT DISHES AND MATS)
PAGES 72 TO 73

"MICE MEAL" AND "GOOD KITTY" DINNERWARE SETS—Curzon Designs, Ltd., 561R Acorn Street, P.O. Box 22, Deer Park, NY 11729, (516) 242-1202
HAUTE FELINE—L. Coffey, Ltd., 4244 Linden Hills Boulevard, Minneapolis, MN 55410, (612) 925-3209
KLIBAN FEEDERS—St. Jon Pet Care Products, 1656 West 240th Street, Harbor City, CA 90710, (213) 326-2720
PLAYFUL CAT SET—Our Best Friends, 97 Albertson Avenue, Albertson, NY 11507, (516) 742-7400
ALL CAT BANDANNAS—Petworthy's, 4 Brookside Place, Westport, CT 06880, (203) 227-0187

WHERE TO PURRCHASE: PLAYING CAT AND MOUSE
(CAT TOYS)
PAGES 74 TO 75

ULTRASUEDE® MICE—Ultramouse, 3433 Bennington Court, Birmingham, MI 48010, (313) 646-8712
CALICO MICE—Haute Feline, L. Coffey, Ltd., 4244 Linden Hills Boulevard, Minneapolis, MN 55410, (612) 925-3209
HIGH-TECH MICE—Petworthy's 4 Brookside Place, Westport, CT 06880, (203) 227-0187
SPACE MOUSE, DRESS-UP MOUSE, CAT FACE, CATNIP TOYS AND CATNIP FOODS—Ethical Products, 216 First Avenue, Newark, NJ 07107, (201) 484-1000
CAT AND MOUSE PUPPETS—A Soft-Hearted Company, 1530 Webster Street, Suite E, Fairfield, CA 94533, (707) 426-3142
SLIPPER AND HEART CATNIP TOYS—Vo-Toys, 400 South Fifth Street, Harrison, NJ 07029, (201) 484-0088

[continued on 49]

PUSSY PIN-UPS!

Paws and Claws (and all the parts in between)!
Order your Burmese Reynolds pin-up poster now!

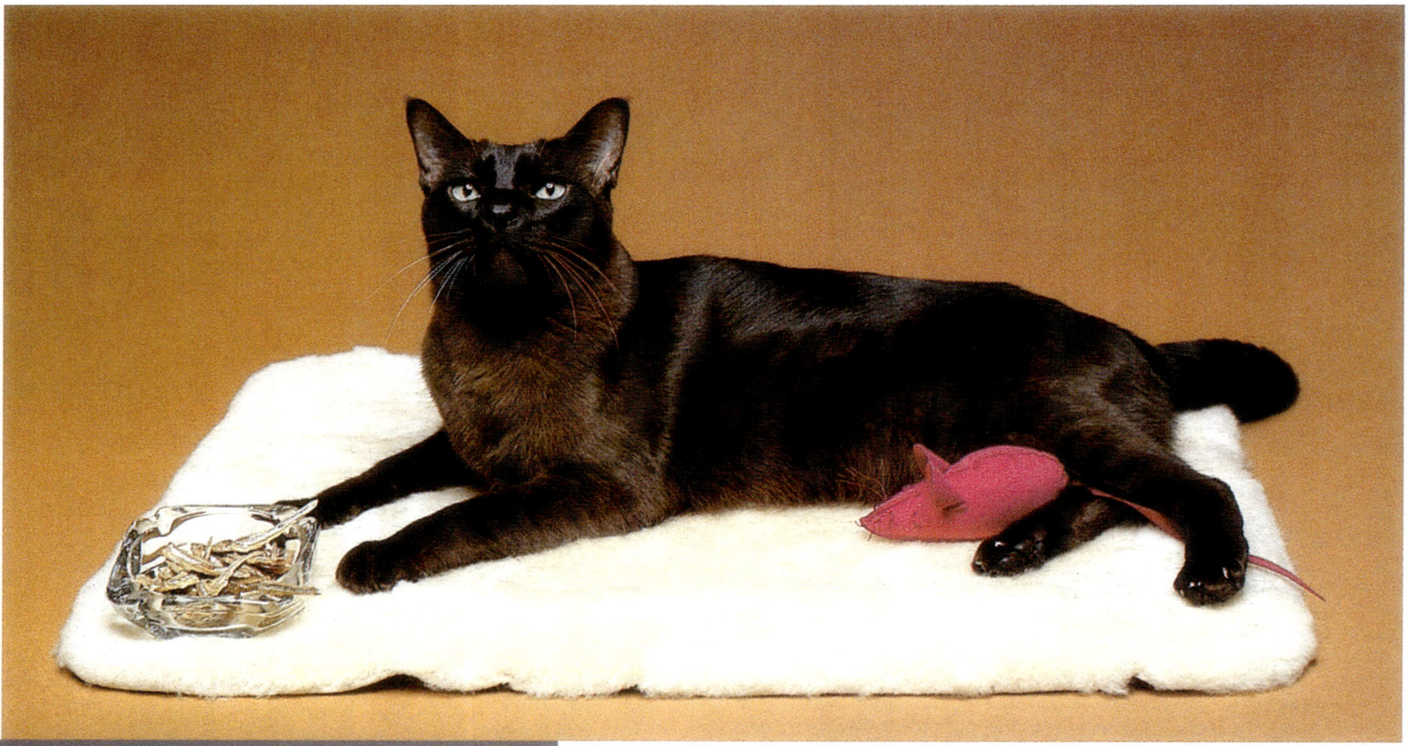

Also available for all you tomcats, exclusively ours, the feline lingerie-clad Furry Faucet-Malayan! The wild tufts of hair you've been dreaming of are here in all their fluffy glory—the fur that made Furry famous!

ORDER FORM

Name______________________________

Address______________________________

City______________________________

State____________________ **Zip**__________

FAT CATS TAKE HEART!
YOU CAN REDUCE YOUR SIZE QUICKLY!

Today—21 pounds

Cat-Ban 3000

promotes the rapid shedding of hair and the elimination of fur balls to reduce your size quickly. Fat cats lose few extra pounds, but are rewarded with great losses of hair and of unwanted inches.

Get slim without dieting. Don't give up a single meal or treat. Don't even move a muscle. Cat-Ban 3000 reduces your size quickly and painlessly with no effort, or your money back. Guaranteed!

NEW

Before—21 pounds

Using Cat-Ban 3000—21 pounds

ORDER NOW & SAVE!

UNCONDITIONAL **100%** MONEYBACK

GUARANTEE

If you do not **reduce your size** with **Cat-Ban 3000**, you probably won't get any smaller unless you **diet**! So don't blame us! Just return the empty bottle, and we will **promptly and cheerfully refund 100% of your money.**

PRIORITY ORDER FORM

Name________________________________

Address______________________________

City_________________________________

State________________________ Zip___________

COMING NEXT ISSUE
CATMOPOLITAN

MOUSE AND GARDEN. Is your awareness of flora and fauna limited to cattails and pussy willows? The clever CATMO Cat knows that her garden can be used to attract more than mice! Set the stage for romance by cultivating catnip where it counts—in your own backyard!

THERE'S NO BUSINESS LIKE SHOW BUSINESS. CATMO looks behind the scenes on the cat-show circuit. More than good looks and glamour goes into the quest for The Best of the Best.

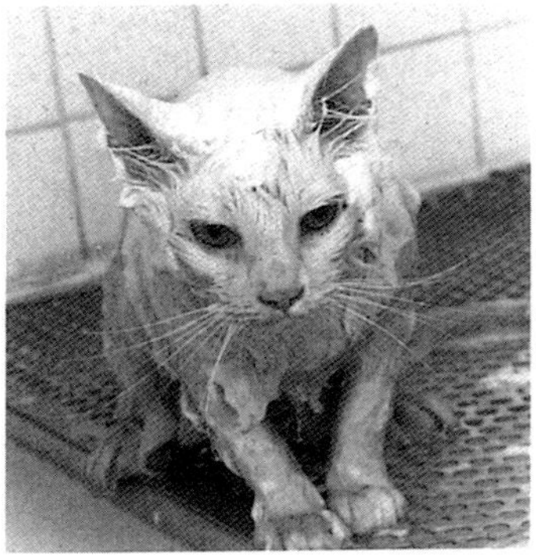

I'M GONNA WASH THAT FLEA RIGHT OUT OF MY HAIR. . . . Your coat collecting critters? CATMO offers a four-step plan for flea-free fur. A beauty makeover that will feel as good as it looks!

GINO BEGHE

SUCKER FOR SUSHI—THE FELINE FISH FAD. Do you have a compulsion to catch catfish? Feel tender for tuna? Most cats select seafood and fish as their favorite foods. Find out why in the next issue of CATMO.

FELINE INFIDELITY. Has your tomcat strayed? You are not alone. Studies have shown that most tomcats are unfaithful. How should you react when it happens to you? What to do when your partner's on the prowl. . . .

WHERE TO PURRCHASE: PAWS TO CATCH YOUR BREATH (CATHLETICS)
PAGES 34 TO 36

PET-ERCISES TAPE—Petcetera—Abbey Industries, 235 West First Street, Bayonne, NJ 07002, (201) 823-3690
THE HOUSE OF THE MOUSE, THE AMAZEN KITTY MAZE, THE CORK SCRATCHING POST, THE CATNIP LOLLY POP, AND THE CATNIP-FILLED CAT HEAD—R.A.F. Trading Corp., 101 Albany Avenue, Freeport, NY 11520
THE INTERNATIONAL CAT GAMES POSTERS BY DON WELLER—Pet Stuff, Inc., P.O. Box 427, Bradley Beach, NJ 07720, (201) 774-9400

WHERE TO PURRCHASE: COPY CATS (PUSSY PAWTRAITURE)
PAGES 38 TO 41

Mimi Vang Olsen—545 Hudson Street, New York, NY 10014, (212) 675-5410
Friedrich Gross—478 West Broadway, New York, NY 10012, (212) 473-3057
Victoria Nodiff—950 Crater Oak Drive, Calabasas, CA 91302, (818) 716-7990
Gloria Vanderbilt, Gino Beghe, and Al Hirschfeld—all represented by The Margo Feiden Galleries, 75 University Place, New York, NY 10003, (212) 677-5330
Thaddeus Krumeich—20 Rebadam Lane, Southhampton, NY 11968, (516) 283-7140
Laura Dabrowski—Laura D's Folk Art Furniture, 100 Main Street, Brewster, NY 10509, (914) 279-6234
Wynne Gilmore—400 Pacific, San Francisco, CA 94133, (415) 421-3291
Susan Gray—Gray Cats, P.O. Box 3303, New York, NY 10185
Jeff Tritel—Tritel Studios, 19432 Richmar Lane, Grass Valley, CA 95949, (916) 268-1048
Julie Evans—203 West 85th Street, Apt. 52, New York, NY 10024 (212) 496-9007
Jim and Ann Monteith—The Monteith Studio & Gallery, 246 W. Orange Street, Lancaster, PA 17603, (717) 295-4517
Robert Guzman-Forbes—23 Latimer Lane, Simsbury, CT 06070, (203) 651-9020

WHERE TO PURRCHASE: PUSSIES GALORE (FELINE FIGURINES AND CAT COLLECTIBLES)
PAGES 42 TO 43

TYBER KATZ©—P.O. Box 141, Roseburg, OR 97470, (503) 679-9519; also, Tallefson's Gallery of Fine Arts, 115 Locust, Oakland, OR 97462, (503) 459-1819
MARJORY WARREN—The Studio, 1225 Madison Avenue, New York, NY 10128, (212) 876-9777
FITZ AND FLOYD—P.O. Box 815367, Dallas, TX 85381-5367
LOEBER CATS—517 White House Beach, Millsboro, DE 19966, (302) 945-2892
THE FRANKLIN MINT—Franklin Center, PA 19091
DANIEL BROOKS—150 East 77th Street, New York, NY 10021 (212) 861-3556
AUTHENTIC MODELS HOLLAND—38 Hobson Street, Stamford, CT 06902, (203) 323-5559
B. SHACKMAN & COMPANY—85 Fifth Avenue, New York, NY 10003, (212) 989-5162
ADORABLES—Private Showing, P.O. Box 18834, Ft. Worth, TX 76180, (817) 498-6646
BARBARA GALLUP—Totally Topiary, P.O. Box 191, Stockton, NJ 08559

WHERE TO PURRCHASE: CAT SUP
PAGES 46 TO 47

BASKET, CUTTING BOARD, SALAD FORK AND SPOON, AND CERAMIC CAT DISHES—Cats, Cats & More Cats, P.O. Box 270, Monroe, NY 10950
KITTEN SALT & PEPPER SHAKERS AND KITTEN SUGAR AND HONEY JARS—Our Best Friends, 79 Albertson Avenue, Albertson, NY 11507, (516) 742-7400
HAUTE FELINE GOURMET SNACKS FOR CATS—L. Coffey, Ltd., 4244 Linden Hills Boulevard, Minneapolis, MN 55410, (612) 925-3209

[continued on 93]